Butterfly Summer

Butterfly Summer

Anne-Marie Conway

USBORNE

First published in the UK in 2012 by Usborne Publishing Ltd., Usborne House, 83-85 Saffron Hill, London EC1N 8RT, England. www.usborne.com

Text copyright © Anne-Marie Conway, 2012

The right of Anne-Marie Conway to be identified as the author of this work has been asserted by her in accordance with the Copyright, Designs and Patents Act, 1988.

Cover photography: floral decoration by Purestock/Alamy;
Cloud and rippling water by Digital Vision.
Title lettering by Stephen Raw. Butterfly illustrations by Joyce Bee.

The name Usborne and the devices ♀ ⊕ are Trade Marks of Usborne Publishing Ltd.

This is a work of fiction. The characters, incidents, and dialogues are products of the author's imagination and are not to be construed as real. Any resemblance to actual events or persons, living or dead, is entirely coincidental.

A CIP catalogue record for this book is available from the British Library.

ISBN 9781409538592 J MAMJJASOND/12 02507/1

Printed in Reading, Berkshire, UK.

Chapter One

We'd been living in our new house in Oakbridge for just over a week and I hated everything about it. When Mum said we were moving to the country, I'd imagined a pretty, old-fashioned cottage with roses round the door – I got the *old* bit right, but it was dark and gloomy with massive spiders, and cobwebs so thick it was impossible to see light through them. We'd spent every spare minute trying to get it sorted, but it still gave me the creeps.

"New house, new job, new beginning," Mum kept saying, doing her best to sound cheery. But the "new beginning" bit was hard – at least, it was for me.

It was alright for Mum – she'd lived in Oakbridge before I was born so it wasn't really a *new beginning* for her anyway. But I'd barely had time to finish Year Seven before I was packing my old life up in a stack of brown cardboard boxes and leaving everything I knew behind me.

"I still don't get why we had to move here in the first place," I grumbled, sitting down to lunch that first week – pizza *again*, served on an upturned crate. We'd had pizza every day since we arrived. Hot pizza for lunch, and cold leftover pizza for tea. I never thought I could get sick of pizza – but seriously!

Mum looked across at me, frowning. "What do you mean, you don't understand? How many times do I have to keep explaining?"

"I know, I know, 'it's a great job, too good to pass up', but you were happy at your old job, weren't you? And what about me? What am I supposed to do without Laura? And what about my wildlife photography course? You know how much I loved going..."

"Look I'm really sorry, Becky." Mum pressed her fingers to the side of her head as if she was in pain. "I know it's difficult for you, but I'm sure Laura will come and visit later on in the summer, and there'll be loads more opportunities for you to take wildlife photos around here." She started to clear away the pizza. "Jobs like this don't come along very often, you know, not when you get to my age. I'll be *running my own department*. It's a huge step up."

We were so busy those first few days I didn't have much time to think about what I was going to do once Mum actually started her *great new job*. It was the summer holidays – the hottest July on record, the weatherman kept saying – and six empty weeks stretched out in front of me. We weren't connected to the internet yet, and I could barely get a phone signal for long enough to call anyone. Talk about being stuck in the middle of nowhere.

We worked our way through all the big boxes the first weekend we arrived. We'd been unpacking for over three hours solid and I was just about ready to collapse from heat exhaustion when Mum's old friend, Stella, popped by to help us.

"Tracy Miller, I can't believe you're back!" she cried, bursting in and throwing her arms round Mum. "It is *so* good to see you. And you must be the beautiful Becky!" She turned round to face me, grabbing hold of my hands and squeezing them tight.

I shook my head, blushing. No one had ever called me beautiful before. Neat brown hair, a turned-up nose and freckles don't exactly add up to beautiful. Cute maybe – but not beautiful.

"We go back years, your mum and me," Stella went on, her eyes full of mischief. "I've known her since primary school, can you believe...?"

I couldn't imagine my mum at primary school. She was always so sensible and grown up. More like a head teacher than anything else. "Was she naughty?" I asked, knowing what the answer would be. "*Naughty?*" Stella roared. "Scared of her own shadow, your mum. Wouldn't say boo to a goose."

I liked Stella straight away. She was the same age as Mum but she seemed years younger. She had wavy brown hair with white-blonde streaks and she never stopped smiling. She swept into our dark, empty house, filling it with noise and laughter. When she got fed up with unwrapping cups and saucers, and cleaning out cupboards, she put on an old disco CD and danced around the room – grabbing me and Mum in turn and swinging us round until we were dripping with sweat and out of breath.

"It's too hot, Stella," Mum groaned, pushing her away, but I could tell she didn't mind.

"We used to dance all night," cried Stella. "And I don't remember you complaining back then!"

"It was you who used to dance all night," said Mum, laughing. "I was the one trying to drag you home! But I have missed you," she added. "It's been far too long."

"I've missed you too, Trace," said Stella, serious for a moment.

It was great to meet someone from Mum's past. She'd never really talked much about why she left Oakbridge. She split with my dad and moved away before I was born, and any mention of him – or "that time" as she called it – was guaranteed to bring on one of her headaches. I know it sounds weird, but meeting Stella was like getting a tiny step closer to finding out what really happened back then.

"Why don't I ask my son Mack to show you around?" she said to me as she was leaving. "He'll only drive me mad getting under my feet all summer if he stops at home!"

I nodded, smiling, although inside my tummy clenched up. I couldn't imagine going off around the village with some boy I'd never met before.

There were quite a few visitors after that. Stella must've passed the word round that Mum was back. That's the thing with small villages – it doesn't take long for news to spread. At the end of the week, someone called Mrs. Wilson came by from the church. She was small and bony and all buttoned up, even though it was easily the hottest day so far.

"Are the two of you planning to come to church?" she

asked primly, while Mum poured us all a cup of tea. I noticed she'd used the best cups *and* a proper teapot. "There's a very nice service next Sunday if you'd like to attend."

Mum half-nodded. "We'll certainly do our best, although I'm due to start my new job tomorrow and what with all the unpacking and everything..." She trailed off and we sat in silence for a moment.

Mrs. Wilson gave me the creeps big time. There was something sour about her – like she'd eaten too many lemons. She kept staring at me in this really intense way, and when Mum offered her a cookie she muttered something random about gluttony and sin. I could just imagine Laura saying, *What is that lady's problem?* and I had to stop myself from snorting into my cup.

"How do you think you'll like Oakbridge, Becky?" she asked after a bit. "It's not the most exciting place for a girl of your age."

"She'll be fine," said Mum quickly. "It's just the two of us, so Becky's used to her own company, and she'll soon make friends when school starts. I've enrolled her at Farnsbury High; it's supposed to be very good."

Mrs. Wilson sniffed. "There's no discipline these days, not like when I was at school."

When was that then? I felt like saying. *In the Ice Age?*

Mrs. Wilson ended up staying for another cup of tea, prattling on about the house and how old it was and other boring stuff like that. Mum kept looking at her watch and clearing her throat in a really obvious way, but it didn't seem to make the slightest difference.

"I'm pretty sure I've still got some unpacking to do," I said, first chance I got, and escaped upstairs.

I couldn't stand my new room. It was small and dark and airless, even with the window open. But it wasn't the size, or the lack of light that bothered me so much, it was the way it felt. Leaving my old room behind was one of the hardest things about moving; like losing a part of who I was. I tried to explain to Mum but she didn't get it. She said that by the end of the summer I'd be so settled, I wouldn't even remember what my old room looked like.

The night before we moved had been the worst. I'd started to think about all the people who would live in my room after I'd gone, and how it wouldn't be mine any more, and how no one would know I'd spent the first twelve years of my life there. At some point I got up and scratched *Becky Miller* into the window sill. I used an old nail from the back of my door, where my dressing gown used to hang. I spent ages scraping away at the wood until the letters were really deep. I just wanted to make sure a tiny part of me was left behind, even if it was only my name.

I didn't really have any more unpacking to do; it was just an excuse to get away from Mrs. Wilson. I lay on my bed listening to her and Mum talking. They were standing by the front door, and Mrs. Wilson was asking Mum about church again. I couldn't make out what Mum was saying back – her voice was too quiet – but I knew she'd be trying to get rid of her. She'd been really funny about visitors dropping by, apart from Stella. She said it was one of the things she hated most about village life: the way people just assumed they could turn up, without calling first to make sure it was okay.

I found the box that night, much later, after Mrs. Wilson had gone home. It was wedged under Mum's bed with a load of other stuff – it probably got shoved under there when we were unpacking. I was looking for a magazine to read and the only way I could reach the one I wanted was by pulling the box right out.

It looked like one of those old-fashioned jewellery boxes, the kind with music and ballet dancers twirling around inside. It was made of very dark, shiny wood, with the prettiest gold pattern engraved on the lid and a tiny padlock. I ran my hands over the surface. It didn't look new but I was sure I'd never seen it before.

I could hear Mum in the living room. She was ironing her shirt for the morning. She was going to be in charge of a brand-new department at Hartons, this big firm of accountants, so she had to look as smart as possible. I thought about taking the box down, to ask her if I could have it – but I opened it first, just to see if there was anything interesting inside.

I don't know what I expected to find – Mum's old wedding ring maybe, or some earrings I could borrow – but there was nothing in there, not even music and dancers, just a tatty piece of fabric and an old photo. The fabric was soft; bits of thread fraying from the edges. There was a message stitched across the middle: neat little hand-sewn crosses spelling *I LOVE YOU* in faded red cotton. The kind of thing you make when you're at primary school.

I placed it back in the box and picked up the photo. It was small and slightly old-fashioned, and I knew there was something strange about it straight away. It was a picture of Mum lying in a hospital bed with a baby in her arms. A baby girl wrapped in a pink blanket. Mum was smiling at the camera, her eyes shining with excitement. I couldn't believe how young she looked. I didn't think

I'd ever seen her look that young or that happy.

I sat there clutching the photo, a million questions piling up in my head. Because I know about my own birth. Not much, but enough to realize that something was wrong. I know that I came too quickly; that there was no time to get to the hospital. It was the end of June, boiling hot, just like this summer. I was born at home and I stayed at home – the midwife said she'd never seen a baby in so much of a hurry to come out. Just me and Mum, *at home*. No hospital. No pink blanket. Not unless they *made* Mum go to the hospital, after the birth, just to make sure we were both okay? Not unless they made her go and she somehow forgot to tell me?

I turned the photo over, my hand trembling suddenly. There was a date in the top right-hand corner. A date written in Mum's small, neat handwriting. The words and numbers jumped about in front of my eyes and I had to blink a few times to refocus.

April 23rd 1986

Twelve years before I was born.

Chapter Two

I don't know how long I sat there trying to make sense of it all, but at some point I heard Mum come out of the lounge and the light went off downstairs. I dropped the photo back in the box, shoved it under her bed and ran down the hall to my room. I couldn't face Mum right then, not without bursting into tears, or blurting out something stupid.

It was impossible to get to sleep. I lay on top of my covers, thinking about the box, stuffed under Mum's bed, waiting to go off like a bomb. I tried to dream my best falling-asleep dream, but it didn't work. It's the one where there's a knock at the door and I open it to find my dad standing there. His face isn't clear exactly but he says, "Becky Miller, I've been searching for you for the last twelve years!" And I say, "It's okay, Dad, better late than never, eh?" I'm not really sure what he says after that because I'm usually asleep by then.

I've been dreaming the meeting-my-dad dream for as long as I can remember – it never fails to send me off to sleep – sometimes I'm asleep before I've even finished talking to him. But lying there that night in the suffocating heat, the only image I could conjure up was a baby girl wrapped in a soft, pink blanket. Who was she? How could Mum hide something *so* important from me? Keep it secret for all these years?

The next morning, I stayed in bed until I heard her leave for work. I was determined to ask her about the photo, but there was no way I could bring it up just before she set off for the first day at her *important new job*. I was worried she might react really badly; she usually did when I asked her about the past. Or that she might just refuse to tell me anything at all.

As soon as I heard the front door close behind her, I got up and trailed downstairs. There was a note on the kitchen table and some money.

Didn't want to wake you – go and explore the village, but be careful. I'll be home at 5.30. Mum x

The note really annoyed me. How could she write something so normal when she was hiding such a big secret? I turned the piece of paper over and scribbled my own note on the back.

Who is the baby in the photo?

Is she your baby?

Where is she now?

Is she with my dad?

If she is yours, why don't I know about her?

What else don't I know?

I was just getting on to question number seven when the doorbell rang. It was so loud it totally freaked me out. I had this sudden panicky feeling that it might be my dad, I don't know why. I guess it was the whole thing – moving house and finding the photo and being in a strange place by myself. Or maybe it was just because I was so tired.

My mum and dad met in Oakbridge when they were really young. Mum was only sixteen and he was her first proper boyfriend. I had no idea what happened to him after they broke up; whether he stayed in Oakbridge or moved somewhere else. He could have been on Mars for all I knew. But if he *was* still living in the village, I was sure he would've heard that we were back by now.

The bell rang again but I stayed where I was, holding my breath. I could see the door from where I was standing.

Someone was peeking through the letter box. I shrank back so they wouldn't know I was there. It was probably only Stella, or sour Mrs. Wilson from the church, but I couldn't face any visitors. Not this morning.

"Get a grip, Becky," I said out loud, taking a breath to calm myself down. I waited another minute or so and then went out to the hall. There was a scrap of paper lying on the doormat. It was another note. This one was written on lined paper, the kind you get in exercise books, and it said:

Meet me at the Butterfly Garden – any time after eleven this morning.

I peered through the window above the front door, but whoever had left it was long gone. I wondered if it was from Stella's son Mack. She said she was going to send him round when she left the other day, but leaving me a note to meet up when we didn't even know each other seemed a bit weird. I had no idea where the Butterfly Garden was for a start – and even if I managed to find it, how would I know who he was?

I got busy in the kitchen tidying up a bit for Mum, but even with the radio on, the house felt too quiet. I couldn't stop thinking about the photo. I'd always longed for a sister. I used to nag Mum about it all the time, as if she could pop out and buy one from the shops, or make one appear *just like that*. She wasn't even *with* my dad by then, but I still thought she could somehow magic a baby out of thin air.

It was just that I hated being an only child; it was so lonely – especially since we'd moved. When I'm older I'm going to have a massive family. I want at least four children, two girls and two boys, and loads of pets. I want dogs and cats and rabbits and maybe even a bird. I want my house to be filled up with noise and mess and loud, blaring music – the louder the better as far as I'm concerned.

I washed up the dishes and swept the floor, but it was still only half nine – eight hours until Mum was due back from work. Every time I stopped to listen, the silence seemed to grow louder. I had to get out. I knew Mum would have kittens if I went off to meet a total stranger at some random place I'd never been, but what did she expect me to do, stuck here for the entire summer without a single friend? And anyway, Stella seemed so nice, it wasn't as if her son was going to be some crazed psycho-killer.

It didn't take me long to get ready. I stuffed Mum's note *and* the mystery note in my pocket, grabbed my phone and set off just after ten. I started to feel better as soon as I left the house – like I could breathe again. The sun was already high in the sky, but I figured there was still an hour or so to go before it became too unbearable. I stopped in at the Jacksons' village shop to buy a Coke and ask for directions. Mr. and Mrs. Jackson had lived in Oakbridge their entire lives, so I was pretty sure they'd know where the Butterfly Garden was.

Mr. Jackson was at the counter, sorting through some photos of their new grandson Albert. "We're in for another scorcher by the looks of things," he said in his gruff, grizzly-bear voice. He'd said the exact same thing when I'd come in a few days earlier to buy some headache pills for Mum. Mrs. Jackson came bustling out of the back, carrying some tins of soup.

"Hello, my love, how are you getting on with the unpacking?"

"It's more or less sorted," I said. "My mum's starting her new job this morning so I'm going to meet a friend at the Butterfly Garden. Do you know the way from here?"

Mr. and Mrs. Jackson glanced at each other. "The Butterfly Garden, you say?" said Mr. Jackson, frowning slightly. He had one of those small fans facing the till and he kept stooping down so that the air could blow on his face. He stayed there cooling off for a minute while I paid for my Coke, then he shuffled round the counter and led me out of the shop.

"Walk straight past the green," he said slowly, pausing to catch his breath. "Then turn right at Amble Cross and keep going until you come to a tiny lane near the bottom, called Back Lane. The signpost is more or less hidden behind a load of blackberry bushes, but if you follow the bushes all the way round you shouldn't have too many problems finding it."

Oakbridge was so different from where we'd lived before. It was about a hundred times smaller for a start. There was no cinema or big supermarkets or anything like that. So far I'd spotted the Jacksons' shop, a pub called The Eagle's Nest and the church. I knew there was a primary school hiding down one of the lanes, but that seemed to be it, as far as I could tell. No wonder Mum had left the first chance she got.

I'd only taken a few steps towards the green when Mrs. Jackson called out to me. She was standing at the front of the shop, shielding her eyes from the sun. "Look after yourself, love," she said. "Mind yourself near that lake."

I was about to ask her what lake she was talking about – there *was* no lake in Oakbridge, not as far as I'd seen – but she was already back in the shop. And what did she mean, "*mind* yourself"? I started to burn up, even though there was no one there to see. Mum must've told Mrs. Jackson that I can't swim; that I'm terrified of water. Mum can't swim either, she's even worse than me – but it's the one thing I never tell *anyone*. I was so furious I thought I was going to cry for a minute. Mum was obviously better at keeping her own secrets than she was at keeping mine.

Blinking back tears, I stomped off down Amble Cross, squishing myself into the hedges every time a car drove past. The sun beat down, prickling the backs of my knees. Further along, near the bottom of the road, there was a row of old-fashioned cottages, small and neat with little square gardens and lace curtains in the windows. There was something so perfect about them I felt my stomach twist up. I bet the people who lived behind such pretty curtains had no nasty surprises hiding underneath *their* beds.

Mr. Jackson was right. It wasn't difficult to find the Garden. The tiny lane at the end of Amble Cross was more of a pathway than an actual road, and tucked away at the bottom of it was a small cottage with a faded wooden sign at the front:

Welcome to Oakbridge Butterfly Garden.

I'd obviously never been to the Butterfly Garden before – I'd never even been to Oakbridge until we moved here (apart from when I was in my mum's tummy, which doesn't count) – but there was something familiar about the whole place. Something *really* familiar. I shivered in the heat. The cottage and the sign, even the stepping stones leading up to the door...it was all *so* familiar, like a dream, or a faraway memory. I stood there for a moment, trying to understand what it could mean.

And then I went in.

Chapter Three

"**H**ave you been here before?" The lady at the entrance held out a map and some leaflets. She was very old; every inch of her face covered in spidery wrinkles.

I shook my head, half shrugging. "No, I don't think so. No, I'm sure I haven't, although there is something very familiar about it."

"That's funny," she said. "I was just thinking the same about you." She peered at me over her glasses. "Mind you, when you get to my age everyone starts to look familiar."

I smiled to be polite and carried on past, through to the tiny shop selling butterfly souvenirs and ice creams.

A different lady, just as old, stamped my hand with a small, red-inked butterfly.

"Entry is free for under fourteens," she explained, "but we do like to keep track of how many people visit each day."

At the back of the shop I saw there was a small door with a sign above it saying Butterfly Garden This Way. I ran my fingers over the inky red butterfly on my hand.

"We've got twenty-four species this summer," the lady went on. "We might even have a Silver-studded Blue."

"Erm, thanks," I said, edging away. And with the map in one hand and my phone in the other, I used my foot to push open the door.

Walking into the Butterfly Garden was like stepping into the Tardis, or waking up in the middle of a Disney movie. It was incredible to think that somewhere so magical and enchanting could be hidden away down a tiny lane in Oakbridge of all places. I couldn't believe Mum never mentioned it when she told me we were moving back here.

Wild, grassy meadows stretched as far as I could see, dotted with flowers so bright they didn't look real. There were old, cobbled paths weaving their way through the tall grasses. And right at the bottom, misty in the early morning sun, was the most beautiful lake I'd ever seen.

I thought of Mrs. Jackson and her warning, and my face grew hot again.

A small yellow butterfly settled for a second on my shoulder and then flew off again. It seemed to be saying *Follow me*, so I chased after it down one of the stony paths. Soon I was surrounded by yellow butterflies and I lost sight of the one I'd been following. I imagined they all belonged to the same family; lots and lots of butterfly brothers and sisters – and a mum and dad who had to find more and more ingenious ways to tell them apart.

I sat down on a bench in the shade and tried to send a text to Laura. I didn't say anything about the photo of the mystery baby, just that I was in the most amazing place and that I missed her. Laura and I have been friends ever since we took up wildlife photography together at the beginning of Year Seven. We'd sailed through the basic module and were just about to start the advanced course when Mum dropped the bombshell that we were moving. I couldn't wait to show Laura the Butterfly Garden when she came to visit. Oakbridge itself might be the most boring village in the universe, but she would absolutely love it here.

A delicate orange and black butterfly landed on a flower by the bench. It was the perfect picture to send with the message. I turned my phone towards the flower as carefully as I could, trying to focus without scaring the butterfly away. It was such a great shot. I held my breath and leaned in even closer.

"Boo!"

A girl jumped in front of my phone, hands on her hips, posing for the picture. She was about my age, with a tangle of long, dark hair and flashing brown eyes.

"Hey, what did you do that for?" I shrank back, closing my phone. "You've scared it away now."

"Oh, you don't want to bother with a boring old Monarch. It's easily the most common butterfly in the Garden." She tossed her hair over her shoulder and fixed me with a stare – challenging me to disagree.

"What are you, an expert or something?" I muttered.

She grinned, nodding. "Yes, I am actually. I know everything about butterflies. Go on, ask me anything you want. I bet you didn't know that butterflies can taste with their feet or that the fastest butterfly can get up to speeds of twelve miles per hour. And do you know what the Ancient Greeks used to believe?" She paused dramatically, leaning towards me. "That butterflies represent the souls of the dead."

I sat there, speechless. I mean, what could I say to that? There was something wild about her, standing in front of me, wearing a faded blue sundress, her skin golden-brown.

Like she'd already spent weeks and weeks outdoors, even though the holidays had only just started.

"I'm Rosa May by the way," she went on. "Also known as Fish."

"Why Fish?" I said, finding my voice finally.

She pulled me up from the bench. "Come on, I'll show you!" She literally dragged me towards the lake, laughing as she tore through the long grass. I pulled back, shaking her hand off my arm.

"What's the matter?" She turned back and grabbed me again. "What are you waiting for?"

I hesitated for a second, and then I let her pull me along. I don't know why – she was just so forceful. We ran together for a bit and then she raced ahead, her hair streaming out behind her. She ran all the way down to the edge of the lake and dived straight in without stopping. I caught up and then took a few steps back. What was she *doing*? No one else was swimming.

I clutched my side, out of breath, waiting for her to come up, but the water was still, not even a ripple. I looked around. There were a few people wandering past, but I wasn't sure if anyone else had even noticed. I didn't know what to do.

"Come on," I said quietly. It was taking too long. "Come on." I began to feel sick. "Come *on*!" I said a bit louder, my voice panicky, and then all of a sudden she was there, surging up from the bottom of the lake, water spraying in every direction as she broke the surface.

"It's beautiful!" she called out. "Why don't you come in?" I shook my head, feeling dizzy, and stepped back from the edge.

"I'm meeting someone," I called. "See you around."

I started to head back the way we'd come, anxious to get away, but she was out of the water and by my side in seconds. "Wait a sec, slow down! You haven't even told me your name." She stopped suddenly and bent over, shaking her head like a dog.

"Watch it, you're splashing me!"

"It's only water! Hey, you're not like that witch in *The Wizard of Oz*, are you? You're not going to melt in a puddle at my feet?"

"Of course I'm not going to melt; I just don't want to get wet!"

She linked her arm through mine, laughing, as if we were old friends. "I was just cooling you down, silly!"

I unlinked my arm and stared at her. "What were you *doing* back there in the lake? Does everyone just dive in when it's hot?"

"Not *everyone*, but then not everyone swims as well as me," she boasted.

"But why did you stay under so long? Are you in training for something?"

Her eyes lit up. "Yes I am! Well, not in training *exactly*, I'm just trying to beat my own personal best. Three minutes was my limit last summer, but I'm aiming for four this year. Who are you supposed to be meeting anyway?"

We were back at the bench. I sat down and fished the note out of my pocket. "This came through my door this morning," I said, showing her. "We've only just moved here and I think it's from this boy, Mack, but I'm not sure."

"Ooh, a *date*!" Rosa May cried. "Why didn't you say? What does he look like?"

I shrugged, feeling a bit silly. "I don't know; I've never met him."

"You're kidding! A *blind* date! You mean you've come here to meet someone you don't even know? I love it! Let's sit here and see if we can spot him. If you've never met each other, he won't know which one of us is you."

We sat on the bench, chatting. I wasn't sure about tricking Mack, but it was nice to have someone else to talk to after being stuck in the house with Mum all week. Rosa May explained that her dad had set up the Butterfly Education Centre on the other side of the Garden, where children came to learn about life cycles and butterfly habitats and stuff.

"That's why I'm here all the time, especially during the holidays, *and* why I know so much about butterflies. Is this your first time here?"

I nodded. "I don't know anything about butterflies, but I'm really into wildlife photography."

"Oh, where's your camera then? Didn't you bring it?"

"I'm using my new phone; it was a birthday present from my mum." I held it out to show her. "It's supposed to be one of the best camera phones you can get; I think she bought it to make up for the fact we were moving – so I could stay in touch with my friends."

"Cool," said Rosa May, glancing at my phone. "How old were you on your birthday anyway?"

"Twelve."

"Same," she said, and we smiled at each other for a moment.

"Hey, why don't I give you the grand tour!" She leaped up suddenly, skipping off across the grass before I could answer.

"But what about Mack?" I shouted after her, although the more time I spent with Rosa May, the less I felt like meeting up with him.

The afternoon soon disappeared. Rosa May showed me all the different areas of the Garden: the wild-flower meadows that stretched for miles, the thick patches of nettles dotted with shiny red ladybirds. She showed me how the butterflies laid their eggs on the underside of leaves – and how they made sure to choose plants that they knew the baby caterpillars would enjoy munching on when they hatched. She pointed out lots of different species and even managed to wait, rather impatiently, while I took some photos.

When it got too hot, we walked over the pretty, arched bridge that crossed the lake and found a shady spot on the other side under some trees. We lay there for ages, chatting about butterflies and boys and how neither of us had ever actually had a proper date. She was so bubbly and confident – not like me at all – jumping from one subject to another as if she couldn't get the words out fast enough. I forgot all about meeting up with Mack. I even forgot about the mystery baby photo for a bit, but then it came back to me, niggling away at the back of my mind.

I couldn't believe it when I looked at my watch and saw it was nearly five o'clock.

"I'd better get back," I said, stretching my arms up over my head. "My mum will send out a search party if I'm not home when she gets in."

Once I'd pulled myself up, I started to hurry. Mum really would send out a search party, and anyway, I needed to ask her about the photo. I was scared, but I had to find out what it meant.

Rosa May was quiet for the first time all day. "You will come back tomorrow, won't you?" she asked, linking arms as we walked back towards the entrance.

"Of course," I said, amazed that I'd made a friend so quickly. "I'll be here by ten, I promise."

She cheered up after that, chatting about the holidays and how great it was to have someone to hang out with at the Garden. "Hey, Becky, have you ever heard of the Silver-studded Blue?" she asked. We'd just crossed the lake and were pushing our way through the long grass.

I shook my head. "Not really, except the old lady in the shop mentioned it when she was stamping my hand. Why? What's so special about it?"

"I'll tell you tomorrow," she teased, "if you're lucky!" And before I could say anything else, she took a small run and dived back into the lake.

"Bye-bye, Fish," I said, smiling to myself – but I turned away quickly so I wouldn't have to see how long it took her to come up.

Chapter Four

I half-ran all the way back, spitting on my hand and rubbing at the red-ink butterfly, smudging it enough so that you couldn't tell what it was. If Mum found out I'd been to the Butterfly Garden, and that there was a lake there, she'd never let me within a mile of the place again. Lakes and swimming pools and beaches were all strictly off limits as far as she was concerned – they were far too dangerous.

Mr. Jackson was sitting outside the front of his shop doing the crossword. He'd taken his shirt off and he had one of those old-man vests underneath. "I'm stuck on four down," he said, lowering the paper and squinting at me in the sun. "*To cast away, leave or desert*. Seven letters, first letter *A*."

I shook my head, shrugging. "Sorry, but I'm rubbish at crosswords."

He closed his eyes, groaning. "Darn heat. How's a man supposed to think?" He used the folded newspaper to fan himself. "How were my directions by the way? Did you find your friend?"

I nodded, smiling, and hurried on. I liked chatting to Mr. Jackson but I really needed to get back.

I was planning to ask Mum about the photo as soon as I got in, but Stella was there.

"We're in the kitchen," she called out as I came through the front door. "Come and see what I got for your mum."

They were sitting at the table, sorting the pieces of a jigsaw puzzle. It was one of those really big ones that take years and years to finish.

"I'll never be able to do it," groaned Mum. "It's got 5,000 pieces and they're nearly *all* blue."

"But you're the puzzle queen, Tracy, my love. That's why I bought it for you. Lots of sky. That was your speciality, wasn't it?"

Mum shook her head, her hands flying over the tiny pieces as she made little piles of blue all over the table.

"She used to spend half her life doing puzzles," said Stella, looking over at me. "She was puzzle-mad for a while, your mum."

"I know," I said.

Mum's head snapped up. "What do you mean, you *know*? I haven't done a puzzle in years. Not since I left Oakbridge."

I shrugged. "I just know. You must've told me once." I turned on the tap and splashed my face with water to cool down. "Why did you stop doing them anyway?"

I could feel her eyes on my back. "Look at the state of you!" she said, changing the subject. "Where have you been all day? You're covered in grass."

"She's just been out having fun, eh, Becky?" Stella winked at me, grinning. "It's too bloomin' hot to do anything else except lie in the grass on a day like this."

I sat down at the table and scooped up a pile of puzzle pieces to sort. The picture on the box was of a field of scarlet poppies with lots and lots of sky, some of it deep blue, some lighter blue and some cloudy. "I'll start separating the red pieces," I said, "but I'm starving, Mum. I haven't eaten anything since breakfast."

Mum got busy heating some baked beans on the stove. She'd changed out of her suit into an old sundress and her hair was scraped back off her face. I tried to imagine her young and happy, like in the photo, but it was impossible. "How was work?" I asked. "Did it take you long to get there?"

She pulled a face. "The journey was fine but the rest of the day was a bit daunting to be honest. The people seem really nice but I've never been in that position before, you know, *in charge*. It's all so different from what I'm used to. I spent most of the day trying to remember everyone's names."

"Well it's only the first day," I said. "I'm sure it'll be better tomorrow."

"I just hope I wasn't too timid," she went on, her voice getting higher. "I mean, I am supposed to be heading up the department but I thought it would be best to ease myself in slowly, if you know what I mean."

"Yes, but you must assert yourself, Trace," said Stella. "Show them who's boss!"

I couldn't imagine my mum showing anyone she was boss. She was the sort of person who said sorry if someone pushed in front of her to get on the bus.

"Oh, I don't know," she sighed, stirring the beans. "I suppose you're right..."

"Of course I'm right! It's like I always say to my Mack, *No one's going to believe in you if you don't believe in yourself.* Not that he listens, mind."

"He didn't come over here this morning, did he?" I asked, blushing a bit. "Only someone rang the bell..." I bit my lip, embarrassed.

"Not this morning, love. He's staying with his dad for a couple of days. They've gone camping. Male bonding or something, his dad said." She roared with laughter, banging her hand on the table. "It's ever since we broke up, he's always dragging poor Mack off for some deep and meaningful experience that's supposed to bring them closer. I'll get him to pop over as soon as he gets back, I promise."

I thought about showing them the mystery note, but I didn't want Mum to freak out. If she thought for a second that I'd gone off to meet a total stranger at the Butterfly Garden, she'd probably lock me in my room – or worse, get someone to come and look after me while she was at work. The note must've been for her, or for the people who lived in the house before us.

Stella ended up staying for ages. We all had baked beans on toast with melted cheese, and then she popped down to the pub and bought a bottle of wine for her and Mum to share. I nearly asked Mum about the photo while Stella was at the pub, but I didn't know how long she'd be. I knew I was putting it off, stalling, but I had to be sure it was the right moment.

When Stella got back they ended up having this big discussion about Take That and whether or not they should've let Robbie rejoin the band. They jabbered on about it for ages and then Mum dug out an old CD and they sang every song, getting louder and louder, waving their wine glasses in the air. I tried to listen and look interested, but inside my stomach was churning over. It was great being with Stella, but I really needed to talk to Mum alone.

It was after ten by the time she left. The second Mum shut the door behind her, it was as if all the lights had gone off. The house felt dark and empty.

"Isn't Stella brilliant?" sighed Mum. "She's always been such a good friend."

"Why did you lose touch with her?"

Mum shrugged. "I'm not sure, to be honest. I moved away from Oakbridge, and I was busy working and looking after you. It was just one of those things I suppose... I think I'll go up now, though. I'm dead on my feet. It hasn't been the easiest day."

She stopped at the bottom of the stairs, turning back to me.

"You know, I really hope I haven't made a big mistake." She was talking about work, about the new job, but I wondered how many other mistakes she'd made. Like not telling me the truth about her past for a start. I thought about the list in my pocket scribbled on the back of her note. All those questions swirling about in my head. *Who is the baby? Is she my sister? Where is she now? Why don't I know about her?* I followed her up, thinking maybe I could just test the water.

She was in her room, lying across the bed, her arm draped over her eyes. "Turn the light off, would you, love? I think I can feel one of my migraines coming on." I stood by the door, my hand hovering over the switch. The questions seemed difficult suddenly, dangerous even.

"Please, Becky, switch it off." Mum propped herself up to see what I was doing. I opened my mouth but the words got jumbled up. I couldn't figure out the right order, or how to make my voice work properly. "Why did you tell Mrs. Jackson that I can't swim?" was all I managed in the end.

Something flickered across her face. It was there and then it was gone. Fear, or guilt...I'm not sure. She lay back down, rolling over to face the wall. "I'm sorry," she said after a bit. "I really am. We were talking the other day and it just slipped out."

"*Mum! You know I never tell anyone.*"

"I'll make it up to you, Becky," she mumbled, her voice full of sleep. "Honest."

I switched off the light and closed her door. I couldn't ask her about the photo. Not right then.

I found it much harder to fall asleep than Mum. I lay there in the heat, with my eyes closed tight, trying to picture my dad on the doorstep, but something was bugging me. I went through everything that had happened since last night: finding the photo, the mystery note, Mrs. Jackson's comment about the lake, meeting Rosa May. I retraced every moment since I found the box hidden under Mum's bed, but I still couldn't grasp what it was. It was like the new puzzle – except the pieces didn't quite fit together. And then, just as I was drifting off to sleep, it came to me.

It was what Rosa May said at the Butterfly Garden when I showed her the note.

You mean you've come here to meet someone you don't even know? That's what she'd said when we were talking about Mack. I flicked on my light, fished the note out of my jeans pocket and smoothed it out in front of me on the bed.

Meet me at the Butterfly Garden – any time after eleven this morning.

It wasn't from Mack, he was away camping. But there was one other person from Oakbridge who might want to meet me. One other person who I didn't know, except in my dreams.

41

My heart started to thump.

It suddenly made perfect sense.

The note had to be from my dad.

Chapter Five

I only know three things about my dad. I was bugging Mum about him on my seventh birthday and in a weak moment she said, "His name is Ben, he's very tall, and he's a conservationist." I didn't know what conservationist meant – I couldn't even say it properly then – but in the dictionary it said, *Someone who works to protect the environment from destruction or pollution*. I remember thinking that was really cool, like he was a superhero or something, off saving the rainforests or making sure that white tigers didn't become extinct.

That was enough for me for a while. I raced around the playground at school, pretending we were in the Amazon together, planting trees and looking after gorillas and other rainforest wildlife. I got a camera when I was nine and I'd crawl around the garden taking pictures of every insect I could find. We were *both* conservationists and we had important work to do.

The adventures we had grew dangerous and exciting, and they saw me right through my time at junior school, but eventually I wanted to know more. Little everyday details like his favourite pudding, and whether he liked cats better, or dogs, and most important of all, if he was ever coming back – but Mum wouldn't tell me. She said that talking about him made her remember stuff that she didn't want to think about any more, and there didn't seem to be anything I could do to change her mind.

She'd already gone to work by the time I got up the next morning. She must've rushed off in a hurry because the kitchen was a mess. The plates were stacked up in the sink with cold, dried-up baked beans stuck to them, and it took me ages to scrub the pan clean. I tidied around the puzzle, leaving the little piles of blue where Mum had left them the night before, and then made myself some toast. The house was deathly quiet again. I sat at the table, thinking about the note, half of me wanting the doorbell to ring and half of me dreading it.

I was tempted to wait in all day, just in case, but I'd

promised Rosa May I'd meet her at ten, and apart from that I really didn't like being in the house by myself. It just felt far too empty. I set out along the lane, past the Jacksons' shop and down to Amble Cross. It was another gorgeous day; the sky so blue it looked as if it had been freshly painted that morning – almost too blue to be true.

I was about halfway to the Garden when my phone vibrated in my pocket. It was a message from Laura. She'd attached a beautiful photo that she'd taken on holiday: it was a spider's web covered in glistening, early-morning dew, with a small spider sitting in the middle. I texted straight back to say that the signal in Oakbridge was rubbish – the spiders miles bigger – and that I'd discovered an amazing place for when she came to visit.

"Back again?" said the wrinkly lady at the entrance. "We do like to see young people using the Garden. I'm Maggie, by the way, and the lady in the shop is my sister Joan.

"I'm Becky," I said shyly. "I only moved to Oakbridge a few weeks ago."

She smiled, waving me through to the tiny shop where Joan was ready with her stamp.

"Have I told you about the number of species we've got this summer?" she asked as I held out my hand. "It's the heat, you see – we've never seen anything like it!"

I nodded, edging towards the door, impatient to see Rosa May. "I'd better go, I'm meeting my friend."

"Oh good!" said Joan. "That'll be so much more fun than wandering around by yourself."

I spotted Rosa May long before she realized I was there. She was up on the bridge, her knees bent, poised to dive into the lake. I stood and watched – she was so graceful, swooping down towards the water like some sort of exotic bird. I waited for her to come up. I knew she'd stay under for as long as she could, testing her lungs to the absolute limit. I closed my eyes for a second, counting. "*One... two...three...four...*" The words came out as a whisper. The longer she stayed under, the harder I found it to breathe.

After what felt like an age, she broke the surface, and as soon as she saw me, she began swimming towards the bank. I raced across the field towards her as she pulled herself out, the water shimmering on her skin like tiny diamond droplets.

"Hey, Becky. Did you see? I broke my record. Three-and-a-half minutes without breathing. Actually, I have no idea if it really was three-and-a-half because I can't time myself properly, but I was counting in my head."

I forced the air back into my lungs. "Are you sure it was only three-and-a-half? It felt more like ten to me."

"*Ten?* I'd be dead if it was ten! Why don't you come in with me?" She grabbed my arm. "Come on, it's so refreshing. We could time each other."

I yanked my arm away and sat down. "I don't want to right now. Anyway, I thought you were going to tell me about the Silver-studded Blue, remember?"

She flopped down next to me on the grass. "I'm so happy you're here. I was sure you'd forget or find something better to do."

"Of course I wouldn't forget – but stop changing the subject! You promised you'd tell me, and the old lady in the shop mentioned it as well. So what is it? A butterfly?"

"Not *any* old butterfly," she said dramatically. "The Silver-studded Blue is the rarest butterfly in the Garden. It only lives for two months a year, July and August."

"So you mean we might find one this summer?"

"We might, but we'd have to be very lucky." She lay back in the grass, spreading her wet hair out behind her. "There's a story about the Silver-studded Blue. I don't know if you'd call it a rumour or an old wives' tale. Some people say it's an ancient myth."

I lay down next to her and we rolled in to face each other. Up close, she was so vivid I had to close my eyes for a second.

"What is it? What do they say?"

"They say that if you spot the first Silver-studded Blue of the summer then the person you love the most is on their way to see you. But..." She paused, looking serious for a moment. "If it lands on your shoulder, then that person has come to say goodbye for ever."

My eyes widened. "No way! Has anyone spotted one yet this year?"

She sat up suddenly, staring out across the lake. "Not here at this Garden. I've been searching for years, every summer."

"Let's make it our mission then," I said. "Let's make a pact to spot the first Silver-studded Blue."

Rosa May laughed. "Yes, let's make a pact. A special promise." She held up her hands and we laced our fingers together so that it was impossible to see where her hands started and mine ended.

"So who's the person you love the most then, Becky?" she teased. "It's not that boy Mack, is it?"

"Don't be silly. I haven't even met him yet." I thought about showing her the note again, explaining about my dad and how he might still be living in Oakbridge. That maybe *he* was on his way to see me. Say the whole theory out loud to see if it felt as real and logical as it had last night in bed – but I couldn't.

"We need to find out everything about the Silver-studded Blue," I said instead. "Where they like to fly and which flowers they're attracted to. I bet you know loads already, don't you? Are they beautiful?"

"Very," said Rosa May. "Deep blue with delicate silver edging around their wings, and more fragile than you can imagine."

"Come on then, let's get going straight away." I pulled her up, excited. "Let's cross the bridge and start at the back. I swear I saw a blue butterfly there yesterday, I think I took a photo of it..."

Rosa May skipped ahead, giggling. "There are loads of blue butterflies, Becky – all different species. The Common Blue and the Small Blue for a start."

"How will we know if we see the Silver-studded Blue then?" I ran to catch up.

She grabbed my hand, smiling mysteriously. "We just will. Trust me."

We spent the rest of the day searching for *ants* rather than butterflies. Rosa May explained that the female Silver-studded Blues always laid their eggs near to ants' nests because the ants protected the butterfly eggs from predators. It was difficult to imagine how an ant could protect anything, but I really liked the idea of them keeping the eggs safe.

We started on the other side of the bridge where it was

shady, crawling about on all fours in the long grass. Every few minutes one of us would shout, "*ANT ALERT!*" and we'd be off stalking the poor insects like a couple of mad detectives. I kept stopping to take photos. I loved the way the ants looked so busy, as if they knew exactly what they were doing and where they were going. Like they'd made up their minds long in advance and nothing was going to stand in their way.

"Look at these three," Rosa May called out at one point. She was lying flat on her stomach, her chin resting on her hands. "I've been watching them for ages and they're definitely together." I crawled over and lay down facing her, so that our heads were touching. "I bet these two at the front are the parents and this one is their baby." She pointed at the three ants. "Look how they keep stopping so that the baby can catch up. Did you know that ants are such social creatures they can't actually live alone?"

"So what happens to them?" I asked, taking a picture of Rosa May and her little ant family. "What happens to the ones who get lost or separated from their colony?"

"They die," she said, blinking suddenly as if she was going to cry. "Except for the really clever ones," she added. "They *always* find their way back home."

We didn't get very far with our mission but we had a brilliant time. There was something about Rosa May.

I know it sounds strange, but when I was with her, crawling through the grass or just lying on our backs, staring up at the sky, I felt charged up – almost as if there was an electric current passing between us. I was praying I'd be going to the same school as her in September – it would be amazing to start with a ready-made friend – but Rosa May didn't want to talk about it.

"School's for losers," she said, her eyes gleaming. "Life's way too exciting to be stuck indoors all day, learning a load of stuff you'll never need to know!"

I stretched out in the grass, grinning. Hanging out with Rosa May made me feel as if my life might turn out to be exciting too. I'd always been the quiet one, the timid one, the one who watched everyone else having fun, but not any more.

We were still talking as the sun dropped in the sky. It was difficult to tear myself away, but I had to get home. I hadn't left Mum a note or anything, but apart from that, I still needed to talk to her about the photo, however difficult it might be.

We agreed to meet at the Garden early the next morning. Rosa May said she had something special to show me. I pleaded with her to tell me what it was before I left, but she said I'd have to wait. "It'll be worth it," she promised, as we made our way over the bridge and across the field. "Just get here as early as you can."

I hurried out of the Garden and back up Amble Cross, but the closer I got to home, the more uneasy I began to feel. I wasn't sure why – I used to let myself in to an empty house all the time before we moved, but it felt different here, more lonely. I slowed down, taking tiny little pigeon steps as I passed the Jacksons' shop. Mr. Jackson was out front doing his crossword again.

"Need any help?" I offered.

He shook his head. "I've just finished, thanks, Becky, although I never did get that clue I was stuck on yesterday!"

"What was it again?"

"Seven letters, first letter was A. *To cast away, leave or desert.*"

I stood there for a bit, as if I was trying to work it out. Anything to delay going home. "Sorry," I said in the end, shrugging. "I bet it's something really obvious, but my mind's gone blank." I waved goodbye and made my way up the lane to our house, praying Mum would be back even though I could see the car wasn't there.

"I'm home," I called, turning the key in the door. "Mum?" But the house was just as silent and empty as when I'd left.

Chapter Six

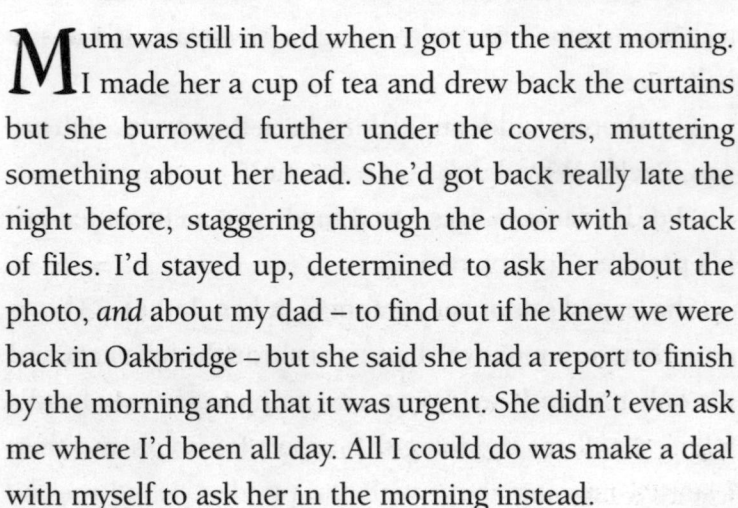

Mum was still in bed when I got up the next morning. I made her a cup of tea and drew back the curtains but she burrowed further under the covers, muttering something about her head. She'd got back really late the night before, staggering through the door with a stack of files. I'd stayed up, determined to ask her about the photo, *and* about my dad – to find out if he knew we were back in Oakbridge – but she said she had a report to finish by the morning and that it was urgent. She didn't even ask me where I'd been all day. All I could do was make a deal with myself to ask her in the morning instead.

I poured myself some cereal and sat in the kitchen,

looking through the pictures I'd taken with Rosa May. I'd got some really good shots of a bright yellow butterfly resting against a jagged green leaf; I think she said it was called a Buttercup. And there was a great one of her little ant family. I was certain she'd been in the shot with them but she must've wriggled out of the way just before I took it. I smiled to myself, thinking about what a brilliant time we'd had.

After a while, I noticed the time – Rosa May would be waiting, but I had to talk to Mum before I left. I popped my head round her door, but she was still fast asleep. The room was hot and stuffy, thick with the smell of sleep.

"Come on, Mum." I leaned over the bed to give her a shake. "Come on, you're going to be so late. It's nearly half nine."

She shot up suddenly, kicking back the covers. "Oh my god, Becky! Why didn't you wake me?"

"I did. I came in ages ago. I made you a cup of tea but it's probably cold by now..."

She leaped out of bed, grabbing at her clothes. "This is a nightmare. I must've slept right through the alarm and it's only my *third* day! What am I going to say? My head's killing me. I was up doing that report for hours and then I started messing about with the puzzle... Hand me my hairbrush, would you?"

"Listen, Mum, I know you're in a hurry, but can I talk to you for a minute? It's really important..."

"Not now, Becky, for goodness' sake, can't you see how late I am? My brush! *Hand me my brush!*" She pushed her arm through her shirtsleeve, hopping into her skirt at the same time, pausing suddenly to look across at me. "What are you up to today?"

"Nothing special, just going down to the green..." I passed her the brush and backed out of the room before she could ask any more questions. I hated lying, but there was no way she'd let me go to the Butterfly Garden by myself, not if she knew about the lake.

It was such a sparkly day, as if the sun had turned everything it touched to gold. I couldn't wait to see Rosa May, to find out what she wanted to show me. I practically ran the whole way. My talk with Mum would have to wait until the weekend, when she had more time. It was so frustrating but there was no point hassling her about my dad, or about the photo, when she was already in such a state about sleeping in.

"Oh hello, Becky," said Maggie as I burst through the door to the Garden. "You're in a hurry! Rush, rush, rush. We saw you taking lots of photos yesterday, wriggling through the grass. Did you get any good shots?"

"Loads," I said. "I'd better go through though –

I'm really late to meet my friend."

"Don't worry about that, you're our very first visitor this morning. It's always quiet first thing."

I was about to explain that Rosa May always came in with her dad, and that they'd probably arrived much earlier than Maggie and Joan, but there wasn't time. Joan was in the shop, holding out her little red stamp. She said she had something to show me, some prints of the Silver-studded Blue.

"You will tell us if you spot one, won't you, dear? It's ever so important."

I promised I would and edged towards the back of the shop, anxious to get through the door and into the Garden before Rosa May gave up on me altogether.

She was waiting on the bridge when I finally got outside. There was a cloud of yellow butterflies above her head, and from a distance she looked like an angel with a golden halo. I was so relieved to see her. I knew we'd only been friends for a few days but I kept expecting her to realize suddenly, that I wasn't quite as much fun as she'd first thought.

I'd never found it that easy to make friends, not with the really popular girls anyway. At my old school, some of them would be friendly as anything one week, and then completely blank me the next. I never understood why, or what the complicated rules of friendship were, but I somehow managed to break them without even trying. Laura was my only proper friend. We both loved photography which was great, but when it came to the other girls in our year – the cool girls – we were always on the outside looking in.

It was different with Rosa May. Not only was she the coolest person I'd ever met, but she seemed just as happy to see me as I was to see her. As soon as she spotted me by the entrance, she flew off the bridge, the halo of butterflies melting into the sky above her. We skipped through the field down to the shadiest area we could find, under some very tall trees, and lay back in the grass. It was warm and the air hummed with insects.

"Have you been here long? My mum overslept and I wanted to make sure she was okay before I left, and then I got stuck with Joan in the shop. What's this special thing then? Remember, yesterday you said you had something special to show me."

Rosa May shrugged as if it was no big deal. "I'll show you later, I promise. But tell me about your mum first. Is she ill?"

"Not really," I said, a bit disappointed – I so wanted to know what the surprise was. "Well, she said her head was hurting, but I think she's just stressed about her new job.

She was up really late finishing an urgent report, and then she slept right through her alarm."

Rosa May sat up, clasping her hands around her knees. "I don't know how anyone can sit in an office, especially on a beautiful day like this. I'm never going to get a job and go to work."

"Don't be silly, you'll have to one day. I'm going to be a wildlife photographer or I might even be a vet. I don't really care, as long as it involves animals."

"But that takes years and years of studying," she said, pulling a face. "How boring would that be? Perhaps I'll get a job right here at the Butterfly Garden like my dad. Then I can spend all my time outside and I won't have to study at all."

"That's a brilliant idea! I know, let's pretend I'm visiting the Garden for the first time today and you're my guide."

Rosa May giggled. "Okay," she said, jumping up. She changed her voice so that it sounded posh and grown-up. "Welcome to the Garden, madam, and how can I help you this morning?"

"Erm..." I looked around, trying to think of a good question. A delicate white butterfly fluttered about between us, landing on Rosa May's shoulder.

"Come on, ask me anything you like," she said. "Ask

me which species of butterfly lives the longest, or how butterflies use camouflage to protect themselves from predators, or – I know – ask me how the first butterflies ever came to be!"

"Okay then," I laughed. "How *did* the first butterfly ever come to be?"

"But that's easy!" she cried. "Haven't you heard of the Papago legend?"

We lay back in the grass and Rosa May began to speak.

"There's a Native American legend, the Papago legend," she said, her voice dreamy now, as if she was staring right into the past. "One day, after the Earth Maker had shaped the world, he sat watching the children play. He saw their joy and youthful beauty and he felt sad as he realized how, as time passed, the children would grow old and die. Their beauty would fade and they would no longer be strong enough to run around in the sunshine. It was such an awful thought that the Earth Maker decided he must make something to help them enjoy life, even as they grew frail and weary. Something that would lift their hearts and spirits..."

Rosa May paused for a minute.

"Come on then, what happened next?"

"This is the good bit," she said. "He took his Bag of Creation, and he put in the blue from the sky and the white from the freshly ground cornmeal. He added the brown of the falling leaves, some spots of sunlight and the green of the pine leaves. He gathered red, orange and purple from the flowers and he put them all in his magic bag.

"Then when he was ready, when all the beauty he could find had been mixed together, he called the Children of the Earth around him and opened the bag. *Behold my new creation!* he cried. *Angels of nature!* And out flew hundreds of exquisite butterflies, each one more colourful than the next."

"What an amazing story," I breathed, rolling in to face her. "Do you believe it's true?"

"Of course! How can you even ask? There's more to that legend actually, but I'll tell you another time."

We spent the rest of the morning roaming the meadows, searching for a Silver-studded Blue. We chased every blue butterfly we saw, wading through the tall, dry grass from one part of the Garden to the next. Rosa May talked non-stop the whole time, teaching me the names of all the butterflies we passed. We saw a Black-veined White, and a Clouded Yellow, an Essex Skipper and a Comma. She told me a little story about each one; their favourite flowers, or how they got their names, to help me remember. We must've seen every species of butterfly *except* the Silver-studded Blue.

Later that afternoon, Rosa May led me down a tiny path running between rows of thick, tangled bushes. The path was so narrow and the bushes so overgrown, it was practically impossible to get through. "Close your eyes for a second, Becky," she ordered, a little way along. "Now keep them closed and no peeking at all." I clasped hold of her hand, stumbling forward a few more steps until she stopped.

"Right, you can open them now, but don't make a sound."

I stood there blinking as the sun hit my eyes. The secret path had taken us into a dusty clearing with a big rock in the middle.

"This is what I was going to show you," she whispered. "When I said I had something special to show you yesterday. This was it."

I took a step towards the rock. It was the most beautiful thing I'd ever seen in my life. The entire surface was covered in a multicoloured velvety blanket of butterflies. It was actually impossible to see the rock at all. I felt strange suddenly, confused, as if the path had led us into a different time; different but familiar. A name bubbled up from somewhere deep inside.

"It's Butterfly Rock," I breathed.

"*What?*"

"That's what it's called: Butterfly Rock."

I turned towards Rosa May. She was staring at me, her face pale.

"How do you know that?" she said. "Who told you? My dad named it for me. It's his favourite area of the garden, but no one else knows it's here. *No one.*"

I shook my head, shrugging. "I must've overheard someone talking about it. Joan in the shop, or someone in the Garden. I'm not really sure, to be honest; the name was just there, in my head." But it was more than that, a fragment of something from long ago. Rosa May was still staring at me.

"Maybe *you* mentioned it?" I said, trying to reassure myself as much as her. "Remember, that first day when you showed me round?"

She nodded slowly, her eyes fixed on mine. "Maybe," she said, but she didn't look convinced.

I took about a hundred photos, tiptoeing right the way round to make sure I caught the rock from every angle. The butterflies fluttered occasionally but they were clearly far too comfortable to bother flying away. Rosa May followed behind me, whispering the different names, and species, and other bits of information, but otherwise she was quiet, deflated, as if I'd ruined her big surprise.

When the heat got too much for us, we left the secret

clearing and hiked back to where we'd started, collapsing down under the trees. I'd packed some sandwiches and fruit but Rosa May said she wasn't hungry.

"It's way too hot to eat. It's too hot to do anything except lie here in the shade or go for a swim." She looked at me, her eyes gleaming suddenly. "I know, let's go swimming together! Come on, I'll race you down to the lake!" She jumped up, pulling my arm. "I'm not kidding, Becky; we're going swimming, *now*!" She was challenging me. Almost as if she knew.

"I'm just eating," I said, shaking her off. "You go for a swim if you want and I'll wait for you here."

"I don't want to go on my own," she said. "Why won't you come in with me? We'd have so much fun. And anyway, I showed you Butterfly Rock, so you owe me." Her voice had changed. She was getting fed up. Losing patience.

"I will," I lied, "just not right now." I felt awful. I would've done anything she wanted, *anything*, except go for a swim. "Listen, why don't I take some photos of you instead?" I pulled out my phone. "I could go up on the bridge and take some really cool shots of you diving in and floating. Or we could even go into the village, to the green. That would be fun, wouldn't it?"

She shrugged, disappointed. "Not as fun as swimming

together. And anyway, I'm not allowed to go into the village. My dad doesn't mind what I do all day as long as I stay in the Garden. He likes to know where I am."

She flopped back down in the grass. "I've never had a proper best friend, you know, Becky. I couldn't stand the girls at my old school. They were all so boring – scared of breaking the rules, sucking up to the teachers all the time. You should've seen them, it drove me half-mad."

I stared at her, mesmerized. "What do you mean your *old* school? Where do you go to school now?" I crossed my fingers, praying it would be Farnsbury High, the school I was due to start at in September.

"I told you yesterday, school's for losers." Her eyes dimmed for a moment, as if she was remembering something sad, but then she shook herself and jumped up.

"Well *I'm* going for a swim, even if you're not!" she said, and before I could say anything she was racing towards the lake, a streak of blue disappearing into the distance. I threw down my sandwich, feeling sick suddenly. I didn't want Rosa May to think I was boring. I was desperate to be her best friend; she was easily the most amazing person I'd ever met in my life. But however desperate I was, however much I wanted her to like me, the one thing I couldn't do was go swimming.

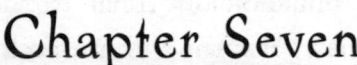

Chapter Seven

Mum was so busy over the next week or so I hardly saw her. She left for work really early, usually before I was up, and got back late into the evening. She said her job was okay, but she seemed to be stressed all the time. She hadn't been shopping for days and she was barely eating, as far as I could tell. It was awful when she came home late. The hours seemed to crawl by and I could never quite relax enough to fall asleep until I heard her key in the door.

I tried to find the right time to ask about the photo, but it was tricky. She was snappy, on edge – either too tired or too busy. I could've just come out with it, told her

I'd found the box under her bed, but every time I had the chance, something made me clam up. The truth is, I was scared. The more I thought about the photo, about what it could mean, the more uneasy I felt.

If the baby in the photo was my sister – and I couldn't really think of any other explanation – then where was she now? Was she with my dad? Did she know about me? It was one thing rehearsing the questions in my head, but what would happen if I actually said them out loud?

I did try asking her about my dad one night, about whether he was still living in Oakbridge, but she freaked out. "Why don't you ask me where he was when I *needed* him, not where he is now? Seriously, Becky, I've got enough on my plate at the moment without you dredging up the past every five minutes. Just drop it, can't you?"

But I didn't want to drop it. I wanted to know everything there was to know about my dad. I wanted to know where he was and what he was doing and if he knew about the baby in the photo. I was *desperate* to know, but Mum was the only one with the answers and she wasn't telling. She's always found it difficult to talk about the past, but she seemed to be even more uptight about it since we moved to Oakbridge.

It didn't seem possible, but the temperature actually

climbed a couple of degrees each day. You could feel the heat pressing down like a heavy blanket. I spent as much time as I could at the Butterfly Garden with Rosa May, hunting for the Silver-studded Blue. We came up with a different plan every day, searching for ants and eggs along the way. We were so caught up in our quest that we hardly noticed the time slip by. Stella kept promising Mack would drop by to show me round, but I guess he was too busy with his own mates. I wasn't all that bothered to be honest. I was having such a brilliant time with Rosa May; I didn't feel as if I needed anyone else.

Sometimes we'd abandon the hunt altogether and make up games to play. We'd choose a colour – say, orange – and then see how many orange butterflies we could spot in a five-minute period. Or we'd pick one particular butterfly and follow it wherever it flew for as long as possible until we lost sight of it again. And when we weren't butterfly hunting, or playing games, we'd lie in the tall grass, talking.

I talked to Rosa May more in those first few weeks than I'd ever talked to anyone. There was something so intense about the time we spent together. Laura and I used to talk, obviously, but this was different. Rosa May wanted to know everything about me; school, friends, family. She hung on every word as if she couldn't bear to miss a single detail. I told her all about my life before we moved to Oakbridge. About Mum and her headaches and how stressed she was, especially since she started her new job. I even told her about my dad. Not much. Just that I'd never met him.

"That must be hard," she said. "I'm really close to my dad, I always have been. There's a kind of special connection between us."

I smiled but my stomach felt hollow, like when you're starving but you don't know what to eat. A gaping hole that nothing could fill. She was so lucky, I don't think she even realized.

She was usually in the lake when I arrived, gliding through the water or floating on her back, her arms and legs spread out like a star. She kept on at me to swim with her but I didn't even like watching – particularly when she disappeared underwater, holding her breath for minutes at a time. Sometimes I think she did it to wind me up – not to be mean or anything, but just to show me what I was missing.

"You're not scared of the water, are you, Becky?" she asked me one Saturday afternoon. We were lying under the trees, talking about the heat and trying to work out how many days had passed since it last rained.

"Of course I'm not scared."

"I wish you'd stop being such a wimp then, and come in with me!"

"I am *not* a wimp!" I rolled onto my front, pulling at the grass, willing her to change the subject.

"*Please*, Becky. Just a quick dip. I'll be your best friend for ever."

I curled my hands into fists. "For goodness' sake, stop banging on about it all the time! Just because *you* swim like a fish! I don't even like swimming. I'm not scared of it, I just don't *like* it!"

"*Okay, I get the message!*" she shouted back. "I thought it would be fun, that's all."

She turned away from me. Neither of us spoke. The thrumming of insects rose to fill the silence between us.

"We could always do something else," I said after a bit, trying to get her to look back round. "Why don't we search for ants? Or you could pretend to be my guide again – tell me the rest of that amazing legend. Remember?"

She didn't say anything – she just lay there. "Look, I'm really sorry. Come on, Rosa May." I'd never seen her so upset. It was like the sun had gone in.

"Hey, Rosa May, do you want to know a secret?" I said, desperate to get a reaction.

She peered over her shoulder. "You haven't got a secret. You're just saying that."

"I'm not, seriously. It's about my mum."

She spun right round. "Does anyone else know?"

"No one. Cross my heart and hope to die."

We locked eyes. My heart was hammering in my chest. I swallowed hard and started to speak before I could change my mind.

"A couple of weeks ago, the day before I met you actually, I found this box under my mum's bed and there was a photo inside."

Her eyes widened. "A photo of what?"

"My mum," I said. I hesitated for a moment. "With a baby."

"What baby? Was it you?"

"No, it definitely wasn't me. And before you ask, it couldn't be. It was taken twelve years before I was born."

It sounded even worse saying it out loud. A secret baby. My mum's secret baby.

"Are you sure, Becky?"

I nodded, tears welling up.

"And does she know you've seen it?"

I shook my head. "No one knows. I want to tell her but I'm scared. She's kept it hidden from me for all these years and I keep thinking about what that could mean. She's always found it difficult to talk about my dad, about what happened before I was born, but this is something else."

Rosa May was quiet for a long time. The words floated around above us. I closed my eyes to make them disappear.

"I don't think you should say anything," she said in the end. She sat up, agitated. "I mean, think about it, Becky. If she's lied to you about something so important, kept it secret *all* these years, she might be hiding all sorts of other stuff."

"But I can't bear it," I said. "I've got to find out the truth. You'd want to know if you had a sister, wouldn't you?"

"Of course I would, but if you force her to talk you might make everything worse. You said yourself that she's in a state, stressed all the time. If you tell her you found the photo, she might be so angry you were looking through her stuff that she grounds you – and if you're grounded we won't be able to see each other any more."

I turned away, shrugging. "I know she's stressed, but she's not that bad."

"Look, I'm serious!" She grabbed my shoulders and turned me back round. "What if the baby died? What if you ask her about it and she can't cope? Swear to me you won't say anything." Her face was so intense for a second it was almost scary, but then she cuddled in close. "Don't tell her, Becky. You're the best friend I've ever had. I'd be lost without you."

I walked home slowly that afternoon, going over and over what Rosa May had said. Her reaction was weird, totally over the top, but maybe she was right. Maybe I would regret it if I forced Mum to talk. Some days it felt as if my life outside the Garden, especially the time I spent with Mum, was just something to get through until Rosa May and I were together again. I didn't want to risk losing her, not for anything.

I popped into the Jacksons' on the way back to buy a drink. Mrs. Jackson was behind the counter, talking to Mrs. Wilson from the church. "Hello, Becky, my love. What do you think of this heat then? We were just saying we don't remember a summer like it. It's playing havoc with my hay fever." As if on cue, she let out a deep wheezy sneeze. "Have you met Mrs. Wilson?" she asked, when she'd recovered. "We've been making the arrangements for little Albert's christening."

I nodded, holding out the money for my lemonade.

"I hope we'll see you at church tomorrow," said Mrs. Wilson. "You *and* your mother. We're a small community here in Oakbridge and we do like to come together once a week to give thanks."

"Erm...I'll ask my mum," I said, edging out of the shop. I hated the way she looked at me, as if there was a nasty smell under her nose. "What time should we come?"

"It starts at ten. Father Hill will be taking the service. So I'll see you both tomorrow then?"

I backed out of the door, nodding, anxious to escape as fast as I could.

The house was empty when I got in. Mum had gone out with Stella for the day, but I was really hoping she'd be back. I sat at the table and fiddled around with the puzzle while I waited. I only managed to do one piece, but it took my mind off things for a bit. I still found the house creepy when I was there by myself – it was something about the silence. It seemed to fill up all the empty space until there was no air left to breathe.

"We had such a good time," said Mum, when she came in. "We went to the new shopping centre in Farnsbury and Stella had me trying on all sorts of outrageous clothes. You should've come, Becky! Honestly, she carries on like we're still teenagers. And look, I bought you this necklace." She handed me a string of purple, hand-painted beads.

"Oh, Mum, it's lovely," I said, slipping it round my neck. "It's my favourite colour as well. Thank you!"

She turned on the radio and sang along while she chopped up some vegetables for tea. It was great to see her so happy for a change. She didn't have any best friends where we lived before. There were a few people she saw from work, but no one she was close to like Stella. I used to think it was normal – that she wasn't really bothered – but maybe there was more to it than that.

"I bumped into Mrs. Wilson this afternoon," I said, picking up a blue jigsaw piece and trying to match it to the piece I'd just done. Mum glanced up. "She wants us to go to church tomorrow. She said something about Father Hill taking the service."

Mum grasped hold of the worktop, swaying slightly.

"What's the matter? I didn't say we'd go. I just said I'd ask you."

"No, it's okay." She steadied herself, reaching for an onion. "We'll go, if you want."

"I don't want to go, I was just mentioning it."

"Make your mind up!" she snapped. "Do you want to go or not?" She carried on chopping, her hand going faster and faster until I could barely see the knife move.

"Calm down, Mum, you're going to hurt yourself! Why are you so upset? Do you know Mrs. Wilson from when you lived here before?"

"No, I don't know her." She was gripping the knife so tight her hand was white. "I've never met her in my life, apart from the day when she came round. It's not Mrs. Wilson, it's just...it's just..." She took a shuddering breath.

"It's just what?"

She stopped chopping, her eyes searching my face. I held my breath. "It's just that when I lived in Oakbridge before...well, what I mean is, the reason I left, the reason I *had* to leave..." She trailed off, staring back down at the chopping board.

"What is it, Mum? Why did you have to leave? Was it because of my dad?"

She shook her head, and started chopping again. Tears were streaming down her face.

"What's the matter? Why are you crying?"

"It's nothing, Becky, really. I'm sorry. It's just this onion, it's so bloody strong." She wiped her eyes on her sleeve. "We'll go to church tomorrow if that's what you want."

It was so hot that night, I ended up in Mum's bed. Her room was slightly cooler than mine and I'd been trying to get to sleep for ages. I used to climb in with her for a cuddle all the time when I was younger but I hadn't done it in years.

"This is nice," she said, rolling over to give me a hug. We lay in the dark for a bit. I could tell she was still awake by her breathing, but neither of us said anything. It was so nice to feel her arms around me. I felt closer to her than I had in ages, as if I could say anything and it wouldn't matter. I don't know why. Maybe because it was the middle of the night and I couldn't see her face.

I kept thinking about earlier, about how she'd been on the verge of saying something about my dad and why she left Oakbridge. I snuggled in, pulling her arms even tighter. "I was just wondering, Mum, I know I've asked you before, but does my dad still live here, in the village?"

Mum stiffened. "Not this again." Her voice was brittle.

"I'm sorry," I mumbled. "I just wanted to know if he's still around, you know, in case I bump into him or something. I've just had the strongest feeling ever since we moved to Oakbridge that he's really close by." It sounded so stupid but I didn't know how else to explain.

Mum was silent for a moment and then she pulled back the covers. "Come on, back to bed. I really don't want to get into this now." She bundled me off the bed and out of the room. "I don't know where your dad is. We're not in touch. I haven't heard from him in years." Even in the dark of the landing, I could see tears welling in her eyes again. "Why are you asking me about this *now*? Why do you keep bringing stuff up?"

"Look, I'm sorry – don't get upset, Mum, *please*."

"What do you mean, 'don't get upset'? I'm working day and night but I still can't keep up with everything they're expecting me to do, and then there's you, with these constant questions about the past." Her face crumpled and she turned away from me, stumbling back into her room. "I'm sorry," she said through the closed door. "We will talk, Becky. We will, but not tonight."

Not tonight. Not right now. Not this minute. Not EVER. Mum was *never* going to tell me about my dad. I sat on the edge of my bed, digging my nails into my palm, so angry I wanted to shake the truth out of her. Shake her and shake her until it came pouring out. Force her to tell me where he was, and why he left, and why she was so determined to keep it all hidden from me.

We both slept in the next morning. I didn't get up until eleven and Mum was still in bed. I threw on some clothes and was halfway through a bowl of cereal when the door bell rang. I was certain it was Mrs. Wilson – that she'd come to see why we hadn't made it to church. I traipsed to the front door, rehearsing excuses in my head as I pulled it open. *My mum wasn't feeling well...we had a late night...we'll definitely come next week...*

But it wasn't Mrs. Wilson at all.

It was a boy.

A really cute boy with floppy brown hair and the cheekiest grin.

"You must be Becky," he said, bowing slightly. "Mack Williams at your service!"

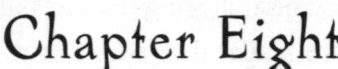

Chapter Eight

Just at that moment I heard Mum's bedroom door open behind me. I leaned forward quickly, blocking Mack's view up the stairs.

"I can't really ask you in or anything, my mum's not feeling very well."

"That's okay," he said. "I've come to show you round Oakbridge. It has so many hidden treasures, you wouldn't believe." He grinned his cheeky grin and I couldn't help smiling back.

"Do you mean right now?"

"Well, right now would be good, unless you've got to wash your hair or take your dog to the vet."

"I haven't got a dog," I said, still grinning.

"Sorted then," he said. "Let's go."

I backed into the hall. "Give me a second; I'll just get my stuff."

Mum emerged from the shadows. "Who's that?" she asked. She was standing at the top of the stairs, her hair mussed up from too much sleep.

"It's just Stella's son, Mack. I'm going for a walk." I grabbed my phone and flip-flops. "Why don't you go back to bed? We've missed church now anyway."

"I wish you wouldn't talk to me like that, Becky. I'm not an invalid."

"Mum, I know. That's not what I meant. Look, I'll see you later."

I slipped out of the door before she could stop me. The last thing I wanted was another row. Mack had crossed to the other side of the lane. He was sitting on a low, drystone wall, playing around with his phone. Stella had mentioned that he was going into Year Nine, but he looked older, tall with really strong arms. My tummy flipped over as he glanced up and caught me staring. I'd never been out with a boy I didn't know, not even for a walk.

"Where shall we start?" he said, as I crossed the lane to join him. "The village green? Or how about the village green?" He spread his arms out wide. "The choices are endless!"

"Anywhere except for the church," I said hurriedly. "I don't want to risk bumping into Mrs. Wilson."

"Ah, the lovely Mrs. Wilson." He smiled. "I bet you didn't know that in her spare time Mrs. Wilson is in charge of the local rugby team. Trains them up and everything."

"No she doesn't," I said, laughing.

Mack laughed as well. "You're right, she doesn't – but I have heard rumours that she goes into people's houses to cast out demons."

"What, you mean, like, *exorcisms*? The same Mrs. Wilson who keeps asking me to go to church?" I wrapped my arms around myself, shuddering. No wonder she was so creepy. She'd probably come over that time to check things out – see if there were any evil spirits to get rid of.

"Earth to Becky." Mack waved his hand in front of my face.

"Sorry, that freaked me out a bit. It's just that I'm scared of spirits and haunted houses and stuff like that, and I *hate* horror movies." I glanced up at him, embarrassed. I probably sounded like the world's biggest wimp. "What do you do around here then?" I said quickly, to change the subject. "Do you play rugby?"

"Yep. Every Saturday morning." He flexed his arms like a bodybuilder. "Training on Saturdays and matches on Sundays – but not in this sort of heat."

We set off from the green, trailing up one of the small, winding lanes. The sun was high in the sky and burning hot. I'd always been shy around boys. At my old school, the cool guys were a million miles out of reach. They were so in love with themselves, they'd never pay the slightest attention to someone like me. But Mack seemed different. He was cool and very cute, but he made me laugh.

We criss-crossed our way around Oakbridge, past the village hall and across a field of sheep. I was more than happy to let Mack lead the way as long as we didn't end up at the church. He chatted on as if we'd known each other for years – funny stories about school and rugby and life in a small village. He somehow made Oakbridge sound as if it was the most interesting place on earth.

We must've gone round in a massive circle because after an hour or so we ended up back at the green. It was sweltering hot and I was dying for a drink. Mack grabbed my arm and pulled me towards the Jacksons'.

"There's one more place I want to take you, but we'll need provisions."

I pulled back, shaking my arm free. "It's not the

Butterfly Garden, is it?" I couldn't face introducing him to Rosa May. Not today. "I don't mind, it's just that I've been there already. More than once actually."

"No, you're alright," he said. "It's not the Butterfly Garden." He stopped for a second outside the shop. "Watch out for Mrs. Jackson though," he whispered. "I know she looks like a sweet old lady, but she is in fact an undercover spy working for the secret service. Pass me your phone for a minute and I'll give you my number – just in case you ever find yourself in danger."

I rolled my eyes. "I'm going to be in danger? From Mrs. Jackson?"

"Better to be safe than sorry," he said.

Inside the shop, I walked up to the counter with a bottle of water, trying to keep a straight face.

"Hello, Becky, my love," said Mrs. Jackson, smiling her crinkly smile. "I didn't know you and Mack were friends."

"We've only just met," I said, grinning. I felt like I'd been grinning non-stop ever since Mack turned up on the doorstep. "He's showing me around the village."

"Isn't that nice. We missed you at church this morning. And you, Mackie Williams."

Mack held his hands up. "To tell you the truth, Mrs. Jackson, I couldn't make it to the service this morning because I was taking a very important call from the Prime Minister."

"Get away with you," she said.

"I kid you not," said Mack seriously. "But don't ask me what it was about, because if I tell you I'll have to kill you."

Mrs. Jackson's shoulders shook with laughter. "I think the sun's affected your brain," she said. "Why don't you take an ice lolly to cool yourself down – and you take one too, Becky. You deserve it, walking about in this ghastly heat."

Mack led me out around the back of the shop and across the road into a small wooded area. It was slightly cooler there, and as we wove our way through the tall, leafy trees, I felt as if I was in the middle of a fairy tale where absolutely anything might happen. Mack stopped suddenly in front of a den. Tree stumps and old branches and planks of wood nailed together to make a small, secret hideaway.

"Wow, what's this?"

Mack laughed. "*This* is where I come when I need to get away from my nagging mum! I built it years ago with my dad and I'm pretty sure no one else knows it's here. Except for my dad, of course – and now you."

My tummy flipped over again. It was crazy. I was

standing in the middle of a wood with the cutest boy I'd ever met in my life. It should've freaked me out, but for some reason I felt okay. Like I could trust him. We crawled into the den and sat with our knees up, facing each other, finishing our ice lollies. The ground was hard and covered in old leaves and twigs, but it didn't matter.

Mack drew noughts and crosses in the dust with his lolly stick and we played best-of-three and then best-of-five. He won every time, cracking joke after joke to distract me and then accidentally-on-purpose rubbing out the entire grid on the one go I actually came close to beating him.

"I have never met such a cheat in my life!" I cried, grabbing the lolly stick and drawing another grid.

"My mum taught me that, years ago. Always bring the game to a close if you're in danger of losing! Hey, did you know that according to my mum we actually knew each other when we were babies?"

I stared at him.

"In fact you *could* say that this is *The Big Reunion*."

"We couldn't have known each other when we were babies. There's no way. My mum left Oakbridge before I was born."

Mack shrugged as if it was no big deal. "Maybe my mum used to visit your mum then, after she moved. At her new place."

I frowned, racking my brains. Every time I tried to think of the past it was dark and murky, filled with difficult, unanswered questions.

I shook my head. "She can't have. We've never met before, Mack. I'm sure of it."

"I know it's hard to imagine *anyone* forgetting someone like me," he laughed, "but you were probably, like, two months old at the time."

"Big-head!" I swiped him with the lolly stick. "How did your camping trip go, by the way?"

Mack rolled his eyes. "Survival in the wild – my dad's idea of fun. You should've seen us trying to build a fire, it was the biggest joke. We ended up eating cold baked beans out of the tin for three days in a row!"

I smiled but my tummy clenched up. I'd eat cold baked beans out of the tin for the rest of my life if it meant I could go camping with *my* dad. "How often do you see him? Is it only in the holidays?" I looked down, worried I was being too personal, but Mack seemed totally unfazed.

"No, I see him most weekends," he said. "He's really into rugby so he comes to the games, and I see him whenever I go swimming."

My head snapped back up. Not someone else who was mad on swimming!

"He works at the leisure centre in Farnsbury," he went on. "You should come with me next time. I can get you in for free."

"You're alright," I said. "Come on, we should be getting back." My palms were slick with sweat. I don't know what it was about Oakbridge, but it seemed as if everyone was obsessed with swimming. First Rosa May and now Mack. Either that or it was just too hot for anyone to imagine doing anything else.

"You're not turning me down, are you?" said Mack as we made our way out of the woods and back to the green. "It's the hottest summer on record, *ever*, and I'm offering you free entry to a great swimming pool and you're *turning me down*?" He put his hands together, pleading. "Seriously, Becky – I'm going on Thursday with a couple of mates and I need you there to make sure they don't splash me."

"Very funny," I said, but I couldn't help smiling.

"So you'll come then? Go on, it'll be a laugh."

What was I supposed to say? That I'd never been to a swimming pool in my life? That I was terrified of water? That I wanted to learn how to swim more than anything in the whole world?

I nodded and shrugged and shook my head all at the same time.

"Maybe," I said. "I don't know. I'll think about it."

Chapter Nine

My excitement about meeting Mack faded pretty quickly. The more I thought about the time we'd spent together, the more uneasy I felt. It was one thing wandering around Oakbridge, or playing noughts and crosses in his den, but the idea of going swimming, *and* with a load of his friends, made me want to run a mile in the opposite direction. It's not just that I can't swim, it's more this feeling I get whenever I'm near water that something terrible is going to happen.

I lay in bed that night, trying to work out why I was so scared. It's not as if anything bad had ever happened to me. Not around water anyway. We never went on holiday to the beach and Mum never took me for lessons, but I guess somewhere along the line she must've passed her own fear on to me.

In Year Three the rest of my class drove off in a coach every Wednesday afternoon to the local swimming pool – but for some reason I was always excused. I don't know how Mum persuaded them to let me stay behind. I just remember sitting in another class doing a load of boring worksheets while my friends trooped off together, thrilled to be escaping school for a couple of hours.

It suddenly seemed very important to find out why Mum wouldn't let me learn to swim. I'd never questioned it before, but if I'd gone to the lessons back then, I'd be able to swim in the lake with Rosa May and hang out at the pool with Mack – normal things that other people seemed to take for granted. What did Mum actually say to my teacher to convince her I should be allowed to miss swimming every week for a whole year? I decided to ask her in the morning, first thing. She might refuse to talk about the past, especially when it came to my dad, but surely this was something she could help me to understand.

I fell into a deep sleep. In my dreams, I was away camping with my dad and we'd built the most brilliant fire. It was blistering hot, sparks flying everywhere, the heat and smoke making my eyes sting. I was so happy I could've stayed there for ever – but at some point Dad went off to find more wood for the fire. I sat there all alone, the dark closing in on me. I waited for hours, until the fire had burned down to nothing – but he didn't come back. It was as if the night had swallowed him whole.

I woke to the sound of Mum pottering about in the kitchen. I got dressed as fast as I could, determined to ask her about the swimming lessons, but as I was coming downstairs she called out that she was leaving and I heard the door slam shut behind her. I stood in the middle of the kitchen, the silence rising up around me. It felt as if Mum and I were growing further and further apart. She was avoiding me, rushing out of the house, scared I might ask her about my dad.

Something made me look towards the door – I don't know what it was; a shadow, a flicker of movement in the hallway. "Hello?" My voice was high and breathless. "Hello? Is anyone there?" I said again, my heart hammering in my chest. I crept towards the door and flung it open. A bright yellow flyer fluttered down from the letter box to the floor. I could see from where I was standing that it was an advert for a local window cleaner.

I almost laughed out loud. I must've looked so stupid, standing there in an empty room, talking to myself. The house was spooky but it wasn't haunted. There were no evil spirits lurking about here for Mrs. Wilson to cast out, just a few cobwebs and dusty corners. Even so, I decided to give breakfast a miss and set off for the Butterfly Garden earlier than usual. I hadn't seen Rosa May since Saturday and I couldn't wait to tell her about my afternoon with Mack.

She was on the bridge when I arrived. I could see her across the field, standing with her hand shielding her eyes from the sun. I jumped up and down, waving, and she flew off the bridge, charging towards me as if we hadn't seen each other for years.

"Where were you?" she cried. "I waited and waited." She flung her arms around my neck, hugging me hard.

I laughed, pleased to see her. "Not so tight, Rosa May! Hey, let go, I can't breathe!" I prised her arms off me. "Come on, I've got loads to tell you."

We ran though the grass and over the bridge, settling down in our favourite shady spot. It was Monday morning and there was hardly anyone else around. I reached out for Rosa May's hand, feeling almost relieved to be back at the Garden with her.

"So, you'll never guess what happened yesterday," I said. But before I could finish, she snatched her hand away and sat up.

"You'll never guess what happened *here* yesterday," she said. Her voice was tight. She paused for a minute, as if it was difficult to go on. "I'm almost certain I saw a Silver-studded Blue."

"No way!"

"*Yes* way! It's true. I was up on the bridge, waiting for you, when this blue and silver butterfly flew over my head. I followed it round and round, but every time I got close enough to check for sure, it flew on and it was impossible to tell."

"I can't believe I missed it. Where did it go?"

"I don't know, over there somewhere." She waved her hand behind her. "But that's not the point, is it? The point is, if you'd been here we could've headed it off, one on each side. I *needed* you here. It was useless trying to do it alone."

"I'm sorry, Rosa May. I was planning to come but I got to sleep really late and then I slept in and then Mack came over..."

"Mack?" A cloud passed across her face.

"Yes, Mack, you know. The boy I thought I was meeting that first day I met you."

Her eyes were small, hard stones. "I know who you mean, Becky. I just can't believe that you chose seeing him over seeing me."

"I didn't *choose* him, silly. He just turned up out of the blue and offered to show me round Oakbridge. He's really nice, and so cute you wouldn't believe. You can come with us next time if you want."

"So you're seeing him *again*. Like, for a proper date?"

I laughed to lighten the mood. "I doubt it. It's a nightmare. He asked me to go swimming at the leisure centre in Farnsbury with some of his mates, but I said no. Well, I said I'd think about it, but I have thought about it and I'm not going. You know how much I hate swimming."

I could've asked Rosa May to come with us, but imagine how stupid I'd feel when Mack saw what a brilliant swimmer she was – it would be worse than going on my own. Rosa May breathed out as if she was relieved.

"I don't think you should see him again anyway," she said, tossing her hair over her shoulder. "I bet he only came over because it's the summer holidays and he was bored."

"No he didn't. He's really nice." I was fed up of talking about it. I thought she'd be excited, ask me for all the details.

We sat there in silence for a bit and then Rosa May threw her arm round me. "I wasn't being mean, Becky, it's just you know what boys are like." She pulled me down in the grass suddenly, her eyes crossed, her arms and legs flailing out in every direction. "Stay away from me!" she moaned. "I'm part of a very dangerous species called Boy."

I started to laugh. It was impossible to stay cross with her for long. "What are you doing? You're crazy!"

"Beware of Boys!" she cried, rolling on top of me and pinning me down. Her hair fell forward, covering my face. "Beware of the evil species called Boy!" She let go of one hand and began to tickle me all over. I tried to push her off but she was too strong.

"Stop!" I gasped. "Stop! I surrender! I give up!" I was laughing so hard I thought I was going to throw up. "Please, Rosa May, *please*, I can't breathe!"

"Promise then," she said, holding my arms so tight it hurt. "Promise you'll never choose him over me."

"Okay, I promise, just get *off*! It's not funny any more! *Get off me!*"

She rolled off and we lay back in the grass, panting. Her moods could flip so quickly it was scary. I stared up at the sky; it was dazzling blue, like Mum's puzzle, except it went on for ever.

"Do you want to see something amazing?" said Rosa May. "I spotted it early this morning while I was waiting for you and if we're lucky we might still be in time."

She pulled me up and I followed her through the grass, back to the bridge. Sometimes I thought I'd follow her anywhere. "We need to crouch down here," she said, stopping right by the edge of the water. She shuffled forward a bit, pulling me with her, but I shrank back, pressing my toes into the ground.

"Not too close, I don't want to slip." I knew she'd think I was a wimp but I couldn't help it.

She edged closer herself and pointed to an area of grass to her left. "Look," she whispered, "there, hanging on that twig near the ground. Can you see?"

I shook my head, leaning forward as far as I dared, craning my neck.

"Right there," she hissed, pointing again...and suddenly I could see. It was a chrysalis, so transparent I could actually make out the butterfly folded up inside.

"It's ready to come out," said Rosa May. "See how it's pulsating like that? It means any minute now the chrysalis will split open."

I took a tiny step forward and eased myself down onto my tummy. Rosa May did the same, lying next to me.

"It's a Tiger," she said, still whispering. "Bright orange and black to warn off predators."

We lay in the grass by the lake, watching the chrysalis.

I held up my phone, ready to take photos. Nothing happened for a while and then very, very slowly the butterfly began to emerge. The head came first, its antennae uncurling in the morning sun. There was a pause after that, just for a few moments, and then suddenly, in a rush, the body appeared, thrusting itself out of the chrysalis almost in one go. It hung, suspended in mid-air, as its spindly legs tried to make contact with the end of the chrysalis.

I grasped hold of Rosa May's hand. "It's the most incredible thing I've ever seen," I breathed. "A new life starting right before our eyes."

The butterfly stretched out its wings. They looked impossibly fragile and I held my breath as a tiny breeze caught it by surprise.

"Don't worry," said Rosa May. "Its wings are much stronger than they look – or they will be very soon."

We lay there together in the grass until the butterfly took its first feeble flight. It was like watching the greatest magic trick in the world; a grubby little caterpillar turning into a beautiful butterfly. I took some amazing shots, recording everything from the second the butterfly emerged from its chrysalis until its wings were strong enough for it to fly. I turned to take one of Rosa May, her eyes wide as she watched the flame-coloured butterfly flutter from flower to flower, but she leaped up suddenly, skipping off across the field.

"Come on, Becky!" she cried, calling back to me. "Let's follow it round, see where it goes next!"

Later on, when I was walking home, I kept replaying the moment the butterfly burst out of the chrysalis, fully formed and ready to start its new life. Squashed in one minute, free the next. It gave me a funny feeling in my tummy, like I wanted to break free myself. I started to run down Amble Cross, my arms spread out like wings. I was soaring through the sky, over the marshmallow clouds, high above the fields – light as a feather and free. I flew all the way back to the green, collapsing in a sweaty heap in front of the Jacksons' shop.

"I don't know where you get the energy, running in heat like this," said Mr. Jackson. He was sitting out front in his string vest, the paper open on his lap.

I laughed, still trying to catch my breath. "I've just seen a *real* butterfly emerging from its chrysalis," I said, as if that explained everything. Mr. Jackson smiled and went back to his crossword.

As I came up the lane to our cottage I saw Stella's car parked outside. I wondered if she knew I'd spent yesterday afternoon with Mack and the thought gave me a funny feeling in my tummy all over again. I rushed up the path, pulling my key out of my bag. I was just about to let myself in when I heard Stella's voice from inside. It was hard and angry.

"What do you mean you haven't told her, Tracy? That's the whole reason you came back to Oakbridge in the first place. You've *got* to tell her. However difficult it is, she's got a right to know what happened!"

Chapter Ten

I fumbled with the key, straining to hear what they'd say next. They were talking about the photo. About the baby. They had to be. I'd never heard Mum and Stella argue before. Stella knew something and she obviously thought I should know too. My legs felt weird, as if they'd forgotten what to do, and I had to force myself to walk through the door and into the kitchen.

Mum was sitting at the table; Stella was by the stove facing her. It was almost funny in a way, like one of those freeze-frame scenes we used to do in drama: *Your daughter has just overheard you and your friend talking about a secret from the past. 1...2...3...FREEZE!*

Mum looked as if she might stay frozen for ever, but Stella took a step towards me, her arms stretched out for a hug.

"Hello, Becky, my love. Have you had a nice day? Your mum and I were just having a little chat." She glanced at Mum, but it was as if she'd turned to stone. "Come on, Tracy. Becky's here and you've got something to tell her, *haven't you*."

I stared past Stella at Mum.

"I've left my job," she said, her lips barely moving. "I wasn't going to say anything but Stella said you had a right to know."

There was something else too, there had to be. I glanced back at Stella, willing her to challenge Mum. To *force* her to tell me everything.

"I'll be off then," said Stella stiffly.

"No, don't go yet," I cried. "I'll make a cup of tea, or some lemonade. *Please*, Stella." But she grabbed her bag and keys and made for the door.

"I'll see you soon, Becky, my sweet. You come over to my place any time you want. And I mean that."

She gave Mum one last long look and swept out. It was hopeless. Mum would never tell me the truth without Stella there to make her.

"I'm sorry," she said, as soon as the front door closed.

"It was the workload, you see, it just got too much for me. They were very nice about it, but I was totally out of my depth. I felt like I was drowning. I don't want you to worry though, Becky. I'll start looking for something new first thing tomorrow."

"But you've hardly given it any time at all. What's going to happen to us if you don't have a job? Will we even stay in Oakbridge?"

Mum gave a shaky laugh. "Something will turn up, you'll see."

I walked across the kitchen and turned on the kettle. My hand trembled as I pushed in the button. I knew Mum had been struggling at work – that she was snowed under – but I was sure Stella had been talking about something else when she said that I had a right to know what happened. It was the perfect moment to confront Mum. I'd overheard them talking and she knew it.

Who's the baby? Where's my dad? Why are you lying? Three simple questions, but it was my turn to freeze. It was something about the way she was sitting there, as if she might crumble into a million pieces.

"Why am I so scared of water?" I said. It was the wrong question but it seemed a safer place to start. "Did something happen to me? When I was little?"

Mum picked up a piece of blue puzzle, scanning the

small section of sky she'd already done to see where it should go.

"Are you even listening? I want to know why I'm so scared of the water. Why haven't I ever learned how to swim?"

"You never wanted to," she muttered, without looking up.

My hands were itching to shake her. "Yes, but those lessons in Year Three – why didn't I go? Everyone else in my class went. Even Davina Patel, and she was scared of everything. But I stayed back every week, remember?"

"You begged me to let you stay back." She was still trying to fit that stupid piece of blue into the sky.

"*But why?*" I was shouting now. Mum was doing what she always did – closing up, shutting down. Impossible to reach.

"For goodness' sake, Becky! There's no need to raise your voice. I'm sick of you hassling me all the time. I can't cope with it, I told you." She pressed her fingers to the side of her head.

"Not a headache! Don't tell me you've got a headache. *Why do you always do this?* You heard what Stella said. *I've got a right to know!*"

"But I've already told you. We were talking about my job."

"No you weren't. You're lying to me!"

We stared at each other, shocked. It was the bluntest thing I'd ever said to her in my life.

"And I'm going swimming." The words flew out of my mouth before I even knew they were there. "I'm going swimming with Mack and you can't stop me."

That got her attention. She dropped the piece of sky and scraped her chair back, standing up to face me.

"You're not going swimming, Becky Miller. I forbid it." She took a step towards me, folding her arms across her chest.

"And did you forbid it in Year Three as well? Is that why I never went for lessons?" I trawled my mind trying to remember. Was it me who didn't want to go swimming? Or did Mum *stop* me from going? The memories were there, but they were fuzzy, out of reach.

Mum stood her ground. "Of course I didn't forbid it. You begged me to get you out of those lessons. You were terrified."

"But *why*?" I was so angry I wanted to smash something. "Why was I terrified? *Why*?" I blinked back tears. Couldn't she see how much I needed to understand?

"I'm not shifting on this, Becky," was all she said. "You're not going swimming and you're not to see Mack again. Is that clear?"

My shoulders sagged. I was never going to get through to her. It was like trying to get through a locked door without the key. It didn't matter how hard or how many times I banged on it, it was never going to open. But a feeling was growing inside me like a hot ball of fire in my belly. I was sick of being frightened all the time. Of being like Mum. I wanted to learn how to swim. And I wanted Mack to teach me.

I left Mum standing in the kitchen. She could keep as many secrets as she liked – but she couldn't physically stop me from seeing Mack. I tried to text him straight away but there was no signal. Instead I lay in bed, working out what I should say. *Can you give me some swimming lessons? I do want to go swimming but I'll probably need some lessons first.* I didn't want him to think I was asking him out, or that it was a date or anything.

Before we moved to Oakbridge, I'd really liked this boy called Jamie Palmer. Half the girls in school fancied him, including Laura. He never paid us the slightest bit of attention, but it didn't seem to matter back then. He was in Year Nine and totally out of reach. It was enough to moon over him in private, doodling his name on our exercise books, lying in wait just to catch a glimpse as he came out of class or ate his lunch.

I blushed, remembering how we used to argue over

who was going to marry him and how many children we'd have. We'd do this silly thing where we'd spin a bottle and if it stopped facing me then I was the one he loved the most and if it stopped facing Laura it was her. It seemed so babyish suddenly, like playing with Barbies or dressing up.

Halfway through the year he started going out with this beautiful girl called Amira. I took a photo of her once, without her knowing. I pored over it, trying to see what she had that I didn't. I tried to work out if it was her hair, or her eyes or something about the way she smiled. I spent hours in front of the mirror trying to mimic that smile, until my face ached with the effort.

They didn't date for very long. He dumped her for this girl Sascha, and then dumped Sascha for someone else again. Three girls in a month, each one prettier than the last. Laura and I would sit round at hers, swapping bits of gossip. Dissecting every last piece of news: *he was the best kisser. He was the worst kisser. He'd kissed all the girls in Year Nine.* We loved talking about him – convinced it would all be so different if only he'd date one of us...

The next morning I snuck out before Mum woke up, and wandered down the lane, waiting for my phone to come to life. My fingers were all over the place as I asked Mack to meet me at the green on Thursday morning at ten. I pressed *send* before I could change my mind. My heart was about to burst out of my chest. It was only a text, but it was the scariest thing I'd ever done. Mooning over Jamie Palmer was easy – he was never going to notice me in a million years. But this was different.

Seconds later, my phone vibrated. One new message:

What took you so long? See you Thursday. M.

Chapter Eleven

I rushed back home and made Mum a strong, black coffee. The kitchen was a mess, but the most important thing was to get her out of bed so she could start looking for a new job. My heart was still going a million miles an hour as I climbed the stairs to her room. She was curled up under her sheet, her knees all the way into her chest as if she was trying to protect herself from something. It made me want to stretch her out straight just to prove to her that she was safe.

"It's nearly ten," I said, fussing around. I opened the curtains and gave her a little shake. "Come on, Mum. It won't do you any good staying in bed all day."

She groaned, pulling a pillow over her face. "Leave me alone, can't you?" Her voice was thick with sleep. I eased the pillow off her face and wafted the coffee under her nose.

"Come on, Mum. Sit up. *Please*."

She reached out for the mug, her eyes still shut tight, sloshing coffee over the sides.

"Hot!" she gasped, grabbing at the front of her nightie to stop it burning. "Too hot!"

It was nearly lunchtime by the time she was showered, dressed and downstairs. I put her sheets in the wash with her nightie and sat her at the kitchen table with the local paper, open at the jobs section. She'd been through a lot over the past few weeks, but I'd never seen her as bad as this.

"What really happened at Hartons, Mum?" I asked gently. "Did you fall out with someone, or get into trouble over something? It's not like you to give up so easily."

Her eyes filled with tears. "It wasn't just the job, Becky. It's being back here, in Oakbridge. I'm finding it so difficult."

"But why? What are you finding difficult? It's not because we rowed yesterday, is it?"

She shook her head. "Of course not. It's got nothing to do with you, Becky. It's me. I just don't feel right inside."

She took hold of my hand across the table. "It's been wonderful seeing Stella again, *more* than wonderful, and I love being in the country, but there are so many memories..." The tears spilled over.

It was awful; I didn't know what to do. "I just wish you'd tell me what's wrong. I wish you'd trust me. You were so excited about the job. I thought it was this big step up for you."

"It was, and I *was* excited..." She broke off, looking bewildered, as if she really didn't understand why it had all gone wrong. "I'm sorry, Becky. I shouldn't get so upset in front of you." She took a deep, shaky breath, wiping her eyes. "I'm fine, *really*. Why don't you pop out for a bit? Get some fresh air."

I went round the table to give her a hug. I didn't want to leave, not when she was about to open up, talk about the past. "It's okay, Mum. I'll stay and keep you company. We could spend the rest of the day together if you like?"

She held onto me, stroking my hair. "You're such a good girl, but I'm fine, Becky, honestly. You get on and I'll start looking through the paper, I promise."

I ended up running all the way to the Garden, worried about the time, shooting straight past Maggie and through to the little shop. I didn't want Rosa May to have a go at me again.

"You're in a hurry," said Joan. "Is everything okay?" She held out her little red stamp.

"Everything's fine," I panted. "I'm just really late to meet my friend."

She looked confused for a moment, but there was no time to explain. Once Joan got started, it was impossible to get away.

"Where on earth have you been?" cried Rosa May as I burst through the door. She grabbed my arm and pulled me towards the bridge. "I've come up with this brilliant plan and I've been dying to tell you all morning."

"Hey, careful, you're hurting me. I'm sorry I'm late, it's just that my mum's left her job and I didn't want her to spend all day in bed."

"Oh no!" Rosa May slowed down, loosening her grip. "You won't be moving, will you?"

"I hope not. That's why I had to make sure she was up, so she could start looking for something new straight away. She promised me she'd have a go, but she's always promising things..."

"Cheer up, Becky. Your mum might break all her promises but I *never* break mine." She took my hand and laced our fingers together, squeezing them tight. "Remember our pact?"

I nodded, squeezing back. "What's this brilliant plan then?"

She explained the whole thing as we made our way across the field and over the bridge, our hands still laced together.

"My dad once told me that the adult Silver-studded Blue likes to feed off the nectar from a shrub called bell heather, and I've just found out that there's a whole load of it growing right at the back of the Garden."

I always felt funny when Rosa May mentioned her dad – it gave me that hollow feeling in my tummy – but I didn't say anything. "What does the heather look like?"

"It's a sort of pinky-purple colour, with bell-shaped flowers, and very pretty." She started to run suddenly. "Come on, Becky! Today might be the day!"

We found the bell heather growing in a completely deserted part of the Garden and lay down to wait. Hiding away there with Rosa May, it felt as if we were the only two people in the world. I'd never been to her house or met her parents or any of her other friends, but it didn't seem to matter. The Butterfly Garden was our special place; like having a secret no one else could share.

While we watched and waited, I told her about Mum. About how I'd heard Stella shouting at her and that we'd had a really big row. She hung onto every word, her eyes glued to my face as I described exactly what happened. The only thing I didn't tell her was that I'd arranged to meet up with Mack. I really wanted to, but I knew she'd be hurt.

"So do you think they were arguing about the photo?" she asked when I'd finished. "Is that what Stella meant when she said you had a right to know?"

I nodded. "I think so. I can't be sure, but you should've seen the way they froze when I walked in. She must've been discussing it with Stella, and for whatever reason she doesn't want me to know. It's not just the photo either. She won't tell me anything about my dad and every time I ask her she gets one of her awful headaches or collapses in tears. I want to know why they broke up and why he disappeared before I was born, but she just won't go there. It's almost as if she wants to pretend the past never happened."

Rosa May sat up, pulling at the grass around her. "I'm never going to have children," she said quietly.

I pulled her arm. "Don't be silly. You'll change your mind when you're older, I bet you anything."

"No, I won't," she said. "I'll never change my mind." Her voice was rock hard. "Grown-ups always lie to children. They lie and they let them down, and they say they love them but they don't. Not really."

"What about *your* parents?" I asked. "I've never even met your dad and he works right here at the Garden."

"He's too busy," she said. "He doesn't like me to bother him while he's working, and my mum's not around any more."

I looked at her, shocked. "What do you mean?"

She didn't say anything but her eyes glazed over and she started to blink very fast, as if she was trying not to cry.

"Where is she, Rosa May? She's not...*dead*, is she?"

She nodded, turning away, but I pulled her close, wrapping my arms around her. "But why didn't you tell me? All these times I've talked about my mum. Why didn't you say?"

I felt like my heart was going to break for her. I was always moaning about Mum, wishing she could be more like the other mums, more normal, but I knew I'd be lost without her.

"Are you sure you're okay, Rosa May?" I said, stroking her hair. "Do you want to talk about it?"

"I'm fine," she said. Her voice was muffled against my shoulder. "It was such a long time ago. I don't like to think about it."

We didn't spot the Silver-studded Blue that day or the next. We lay on our backs, staring up at the endless blue sky, talking and mucking about. The hours drifted by in a lazy haze of sunshine. We saw lots of blue butterflies, all of them after the sweet bell heather nectar, but none of them had delicate silver edging around their wings.

Early on Wednesday afternoon, we noticed Joan from the souvenir shop coming towards us across the field. I'd never actually seen her outside before, and just for a moment I wondered if something was wrong. As soon as Rosa May realized she was headed our way, she leaped up and hid behind the nearest tree. "*What are you doing?*" I hissed, but she put her finger to her lips to shush me.

"Oh, hello, dear," said Joan a moment later, walking straight past the tree and stopping in front of me. "I really felt the need to stretch my legs, but it's sweltering out here. Is your friend not coming to meet you today?"

I was about to answer when Rosa May slipped out from behind the tree so she was standing directly behind Joan. "Erm...later on th-this afternoon," I stammered, trying not to laugh. "She's...erm...busy at the moment."

Joan began to tell me about her favourite butterfly, the Marbled White, and about how she'd spotted one on the way down to me, while Rosa May waved her arms around behind her, pretending to stamp her hand over and over like Joan does in her little shop. I held my breath to stop myself snorting. She looked so silly I thought I was going to burst.

"Are you okay?" said Joan. "You're ever so red in the face."

I sucked my cheeks in, trying to keep a straight face. I was sure she was going to turn round any second and catch Rosa May. "It's the heat," I spluttered. "I've probably had too much sun." Rosa May stopped stamping her hand and pretended to wipe imaginary sweat from her forehead, swooning back as if she was about to faint.

"It's just that we hate to see you out here on your own," Joan went on. "It can't be much fun." I shook my head, and then nodded, willing her to go before I gave the game away. "Anyway, I'd best be getting on." She turned to go and Rosa May slipped back behind the tree. "I do hope your friend turns up soon."

We waited a minute, until Joan was far enough away, and then collapsed laughing.

"Don't ever do that again!" I gasped. "I thought I was going to die!"

Rosa May rolled around in the grass, clutching her stomach. "But you should've seen your face, Becky! It was classic!"

"Yeah, but Maggie and Joan will think I'm some saddo loser with no friends!"

"So what if they do? They're just two saddo old wrinklies with no life!"

"No they're not!" She was so mean about people sometimes. "Anyway, I think they're sweet."

"*Sweet*," she snorted, leaping up suddenly and pretending to stamp her hand over and over.

I wrestled her back down, laughing again. I don't think I'd ever laughed so much in my life, or had so much fun. "You're off your head," I said, when I managed to get my breath back, "but I love you anyway."

"Love you too, Becky Miller," said Rosa May, and we lay back in the grass, grinning.

Nothing much happened for the rest of the afternoon. I think I'd half given up on ever spotting a Silver-studded Blue. I so wanted to believe in the myth – believe that my dad would be on his way to see me if only I was the first to spot one this summer. But the world was so big and my dad could be anywhere, and if he'd never been interested in finding me before, why would he suddenly show up now?

"Do you know where I think we might be going wrong?" said Rosa May, as I was getting ready to leave. "Some butterflies only like to feed very early in the morning, at sunrise, so if we're going to spot one around the bell heather we probably need to get here much earlier than usual."

I had no idea if that was true or not but I was meeting Mack the next day anyway, so I wouldn't be coming to the Garden at all.

We wandered up through the fields, the sun beating down on our backs. "I wish you didn't have to go yet," she said, hugging me by the exit. "What time do you think you can get here tomorrow?"

I hesitated for a moment. "Erm, I'm not sure, to be honest, Rosa May. I've made other plans."

She pulled away, grabbing hold of my shoulders, her fingers digging in through my T-shirt. "What do you mean? You've got to come. You've *got* to. I'll be waiting for you."

"Well, I'll try, Rosa May, but—"

"But *what*?"

I shrugged helplessly, pushing her arms off. I couldn't tell her about Mack – she'd only think I was choosing him over her. I don't know why she had to be so possessive.

"Look, I'll try to come, but I can't promise it'll be first thing, okay?"

"No, it's not okay actually. I thought we had a pact!"

"We do," I said. "But it's only one day. It's not such a big deal, is it?"

Her eyes narrowed. "It is to me," she said coldly. "Perhaps I won't bother coming either, if that's how you feel." And she spun round and ran off, disappearing into the long, dry grass.

I made my way back to the green feeling horribly guilty. I didn't want to change my plans with Mack, but I didn't want to spoil my friendship with Rosa May either. Even with her funny moods and outbursts, she was still the best friend I'd ever had. I don't know why she was so worried; I'd never let anyone come between us.

It was getting late but I crossed the lane and caught a bus into Farnsbury. If I was going to learn how to swim, I needed to buy myself a swimsuit, and I wasn't going to find one at the Jacksons' village store.

It was the first time I'd left the village since we arrived and I felt as if every person on the bus knew I was up to no good. I sat at the back with my face pressed against the window, trying very hard to remember why I'd wanted to go swimming in the first place. If Mum found out about this of all things, she'd probably ground me for the rest of my life.

I got off the bus in the middle of town. It was so big and noisy compared with Oakbridge; it was as if someone had suddenly turned up the volume on my life. I wandered around for a bit until I found the new shopping centre, the one Mum had been to with Stella. It was a huge silver building with mirrors everywhere and loud music blaring out of every shop. I'd never really been shopping on my own. Laura and I had gone up to the High Road sometimes, to get a milkshake or buy a new CD, but this felt different.

I found a lot of swimsuits, but most of them were skimpy bikinis with frills around the bottoms and tiny triangle tops. I picked them up and dropped them again, my face growing hot. Mum would have a fit if I came home with something like that – not that I was going to show her. In the end, I chose a purple one-piece with a pretty lilac pattern, and left as quickly as I could.

By the time I got back to Oakbridge I'd nearly changed my mind about the whole thing. The ball of fire in my belly had gone and I just felt hollow and scared. Sneaking around behind Mum's back... Lying to Rosa May... Meeting up with a boy I hardly knew... *Swimming*... I was completely out of my depth and I hadn't even got to the pool yet.

The bus stopped just outside the Jacksons' shop. Mr. and Mrs. Jackson were standing in the doorway, sharing a bright orange ice lolly.

"What's the matter, love?" said Mr. Jackson. "You look as if you found a penny and lost a pound."

I half-shrugged, trying to smile. The Jacksons were always so nice to me – they were like the grandparents I'd never had. Mum's parents died before I was born, when she was quite young herself, and I'd never met *anyone* from my dad's family.

"Let me tell you something, Becky," said Mrs. Jackson. "Some words of wisdom from an old lady. It's what I tell Mr. Jackson whenever he gets himself into a state." She smiled up at Mr. Jackson, handing him the lolly. "Worrying about things is like sitting in a rocking chair," she said. "It gives you something to do but it doesn't actually get you anywhere." Her face creased up and she started to laugh her big wheezy laugh. "Do you get it, Becky? All that rocking backwards and forwards, going over and over the same old worries, and at the end of the day you're in exactly the same place as when you started."

"Yes, I get it, Mrs. Jackson, but—"

"She's right, you know," said Mr. Jackson, interrupting me. "You should see the state I get into when I can't finish my crossword! Drives me half round the bend."

I smiled, remembering the clue neither of us could get that day.

"You shouldn't be worrying anyway, a girl your age," he added kindly.

I said thanks and goodbye, then ran all the way home without stopping. I could hear Mr. and Mrs. Jackson laughing as I went. Maybe they were right. Worrying about things wasn't going to help. Mum would find a new job and I'd learn how to swim and everything would be fine.

But when I got in, Mum was in bed *again*. All the windows were closed and the sink was piled high with two days' worth of plates and cups. The only sign she'd been up at all was the puzzle. She'd practically finished the sky; hundreds of tiny blue pieces covering every centimetre of the old, wooden table.

Chapter Twelve

I had the whole journey to Farnsbury to tell Mack I couldn't swim. We were meeting his friends there, so it was just the two of us on the bus, but by the time we arrived I still hadn't said anything. He chatted away, showing me things out of the window and filling me in on what he'd been doing for the past few days, while I sat there rehearsing the words over and over until they didn't even make sense in my own head. Telling someone you can't swim and that you're terrified of water when you're twelve years old felt like the ultimate embarrassment.

"You're going to love this place," he said as we got off the bus. "It's got slides and a wave machine and—"

"Hang on a minute, *wait!*" I pulled his arm. "You didn't say anything about *slides*." My voice was so high-pitched it was practically off the scale. "I don't like slides or wave machines or—"

"Woah! Calm down, Becky, don't stress. There are two pools here – the fun pool and the swimming pool. If it's Olympic swimming you're after, you've come with the right person! I was practically born in a swimming pool. My favourite stroke is the butterfly. Most people can't do it properly, to be honest, but it's all in the breathing."

Mack gabbled on, but I froze, unable to take another step. It was hearing the word "butterfly". Suddenly all I wanted was to be back at the Garden with Rosa May, lying in the grass together, hidden away from the rest of the world. She was probably on the bridge right that minute, waiting for me to arrive – if she'd bothered to show up after our row.

"Earth to Becky! What's the matter?" Mack waved his hand in front of my face.

"Look, I'm sorry but there's something I need to tell you." I swallowed hard. "I know I should've told you before but the thing is, well the problem is, I've never been swimming, so you see I can't really swim, I mean I *want* to learn, but..."

I broke off, totally mortified, my face burning up.

"But that's fantastic!" cried Mack.

"*What?*"

"You see, when I said 'Olympic *swimming*' what I meant to say was 'Olympic swimming *teacher*'. I kid you not, Becky. I might not have the certificates to show for it, but I've never failed to teach someone to swim."

I couldn't believe it, it was too good to be true. "How many people have you actually taught then?" I asked, pressing my hands to my flaming cheeks.

"None yet." He grinned. "But that means I've never failed, right? Come on, I won't make you do anything you're not comfortable with, I promise. Scout's honour."

The leisure centre was on the outskirts of town, next to a bowling alley and cinema. The smell hit me the second we walked in. It was horrible. I had to breathe through my mouth to stop myself retching. And it wasn't just the smell. There was something about the whole place. It was familiar. Like the Butterfly Garden, and Butterfly Rock. That same strange feeling. I'd never been swimming in my life and I'd certainly never been to Farnsbury before yesterday, but somehow I *knew* this place.

Mack's friends were waiting for him just inside – Stevie and Ajay. He introduced me and I tried to smile. They seemed okay but there was no point trying to chat to them, the noise was deafening. It seemed to echo through the entire building. I kept my eyes on the door, ready to run at the first opportunity. There was a queue to pay, but Mack waved a pass at the man behind the desk and he let us straight through.

"The girls' changing rooms are over there," he said. "Meet us back here when you're ready. And seriously, Becky, it's going to be fine. Trust me."

I went off by myself to the changing area, trying to understand how some random leisure centre in Farnsbury could feel so familiar. It wasn't as if I knew where anything was, not specifically, it was just this strong feeling that I'd been here before. It was so weird, like I'd lived two completely separate lives and my other life was somehow leaking into this one. It was seriously beginning to freak me out.

The changing rooms were packed with families. Little children learning to swim, some of them still babies. I changed into my new swimsuit as if I was on automatic pilot and made my way back out to Mack. He was leaning against the railings by the pool, wearing a pair of baggy black shorts. I shuffled over in my old pink flip-flops with my towel clutched round me, literally forcing myself to put one foot in front of the other.

The pool looked huge behind him. Serious swimmers were racing up and down the lanes, their arms slicing through the water like those tools with rotating blades.

"Stevie and Ajay have gone into the other pool to muck about but we can stay here if you want," said Mack as I came over. "Just leave your towel with mine and follow me."

I shuffled after him around the edge of the pool, keeping as far away from the water as possible. The noise seemed to fill up my head until it was difficult to think. Shouting and shrieking and yelling. Even that was familiar, like something you recognize from a terrible dream.

"I'm not actually going in," I shouted over the din. "I'll just watch for today."

Mack stopped at the far end and sat down, his feet dangling in the water. "Come on, sit here next to me." He patted the space beside him. "That's all you need to do for now."

I crouched down next to him, my legs tucked right up so that my feet could stay planted firmly on the side, rather than dangle in the water by his.

"I'll tell you a secret," he said. "I was scared of swimming when I was little. I didn't mind being in the pool so much, the problem was I didn't like getting water in my eyes. My dad used to bring me here all the time and all the big boys used to jump in and splash me and I was terrified."

I glanced up at him. "You're just saying that."

"No, I swear on my life, it's true. They'd do these kamikaze dive-bombs, jumping off the side with their knees tucked up for maximum impact. I used to cry like a baby."

"And was your dad nice about it?"

Mack made a face. "Not really. He said I needed to toughen up, act like a real man."

"He's not here today, is he?" I looked around nervously, half expecting him to run up behind me and push me in – just to toughen *me* up.

Mack shook his head, laughing, and then slid off the side of the pool, disappearing under the water and coming up again almost immediately.

"I just wanted to show you that it's not *that* deep," he said, standing up. "Look, it barely reaches the top of my chest."

"I hope you don't think I'm going to do that."

"Course not," he said. "I told you, we're going to take things very slowly. We've got all summer."

"What do you mean?" I said, my heart flipping over. But he gave me a cheeky grin and pushed away from the side, swimming up the lane, showing off like a real Olympic swimmer. I tried to imagine swimming like that, or even getting into the water, but it was impossible.

I wasn't even brave enough to dip my feet in.

Mack spent the next half an hour or so swimming a few lengths and then coming back over to talk to me, leaning against the edge of the pool, his arms crossed in front of him. Very slowly I began to relax. It was fun chatting and I felt pretty safe sitting on the side. I'd almost forgotten why we were there in the first place when Mack pulled himself out of the water suddenly, squashing up next to me.

"Listen, Becky. There's one thing I want you to do today if you're serious about learning to swim – and I can tell you are by that determined look in your eyes."

I blushed, looking away. I was determined alright. Determined never to come anywhere near a swimming pool ever again.

"What is it? What do you want me to do?"

He slipped back into the pool and turned to face me. "I want you to reach your arms out towards me and I'm going to lower you into the water, holding you all the time. And then I'll lift you out again as soon as you want me to. That's it."

"No, I can't." I shook my head, moving back.

"Seriously, Becky. You've got to trust me. I'm not going to do anything silly. Just put your legs round my waist, hold onto my shoulders and everything will be fine."

It was as if I was in some sort of hypnotic trance. I leaned forward, still shaking my head, as Mack lifted me up and lowered me down into the pool. It was so cold I gasped, grabbing his shoulders and digging my nails in as hard as I could. He didn't even flinch. He just held me in the water, bobbing very gently up and down. I didn't know whether to die of embarrassment or fear.

"Don't drop me," I said. I was nearly in tears.

He pulled a face. "I couldn't even if I wanted to – you've surgically attached yourself to me with your nails." I started to laugh then, but dug my nails in deeper just in case he thought I was okay.

The water lapped against us. Gradually my heart slowed down and I relaxed my grip. It wasn't nice exactly, but I didn't feel as if I was about to die. I kept telling myself that I wasn't born scared, it was just something I'd learned along the way, and Mack kept bouncing very gently, moving me around so that I didn't get too cold.

"You're doing so well, Becky," he said. "In fact you're my best student ever!"

"Your only student, you mean," I said.

"So far," said Mack. "And you see, even if I let go of you – which I won't – nothing would happen because you'd be able to just stand up on your own. It's too shallow for anything to go wrong." He smiled and I could feel myself melt. He was just so nice.

"Next time," I said, surprising myself, "next time we come, I'll stand."

Mum was in the kitchen when I got home. There were dishes everywhere and it was beginning to smell. She was sitting at the table with a piece of red puzzle in her hand.

"Look, I've made a start on the poppies," she said. "They're so much easier than the sky." The sky was finished and there were little piles of red dotted about in front of her. I didn't get too close in case she realized I'd been swimming. My hair was dry but I could still smell the chlorine on my skin. It would've been so great to tell her. To share the day. The secrets between us were growing out of control, like some sort of mutant bacteria.

"Have you called up about any of those jobs in the paper?" I asked. "I mean, the puzzle looks great, but you haven't been doing it all day, have you? Maybe you could even speak to someone at Hartons? See if they have something else you could do."

"Don't start nagging, Becky. I'm not feeling too good. I'll get onto it tomorrow, I promise."

Another promise she wouldn't keep. Mum had changed

so much since we got to Oakbridge. She'd always been secretive about the past, but now it was as if she was disappearing inside herself. She was hiding something from me, something bad, something to do with Oakbridge and my dad and the photo under the bed, and I badly needed to know what it was.

I stopped at the doorway watching her for a moment. She was concentrating on the puzzle, fiddling around with one of the pieces, but her face was as sad as I'd ever seen it. "Mum, I was just wondering, are you sure we never came to Oakbridge, you know, after you moved away?"

She looked up, frowning. "What do you mean?"

"It just seems weird, in a way, that you left and never came back. And I keep getting this feeling..."

"What sort of feeling?"

"I don't know, just a funny feeling. Like certain places in Oakbridge feel so familiar sometimes."

She looked back down at the puzzle. "I never came back here after I left. Not once." Her voice was shaking slightly. "I don't know what you're talking about. You must be imagining things. Where have you been exactly? Where did you get this feeling?"

I shook my head, sighing. "Look, it doesn't matter. Forget it. I'm going up to my room."

I tossed and turned for most of the night – it was so

unbearably hot. I kept thinking about Mack and the pool and the way I felt when I first walked into the building. How could some place I'd never been to feel so familiar? I could never explain to Mum. It was just a sense, a distant recollection, but the noise and the smell – they'd felt as real as if I'd been going there all my life.

It was almost morning by the time I finally dropped off to sleep. I dreamed about my dad. We were swimming underwater and it was completely silent. I was dying to see his face but it was fuzzy and out of focus. I tried to get closer, but no matter how fast I swam he was always that little bit faster. *Keep still, can't you?* I kept thinking. But when I finally caught up and grabbed him by the shoulders to take a proper look, it wasn't my dad at all. It was Rosa May.

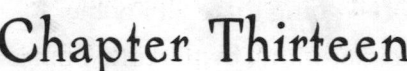

Chapter Thirteen

I woke with a start. I didn't know where I was. That strange feeling when you're still half in your dream. I forced myself out of bed and pulled on a pair of shorts. I was exhausted, but I had to get to the Butterfly Garden as early as possible if I was ever going to spot the Silver-studded Blue. *And* if Rosa May was going to forgive me for not turning up yesterday.

I popped my head round Mum's door just before I left. The room was dark and stuffy. "I'm off now," I said. "Shall I open the curtains for you?" She didn't answer, and as I got a bit closer to give her a kiss, I realized the bed was empty. I turned on the light, confused. It was the first day she'd been up before me since she'd left her job.

Downstairs, the kitchen was still a mess, but it didn't look as if she'd had any breakfast and the kettle was stone cold. She must've crept out at some point, either earlier on, or maybe even late last night. I thought about calling Stella, telling her I was worried, but I didn't want to make a big fuss over nothing. It wasn't as if Mum was a child. In the end I left her a note asking her to ring me as soon as she came in. She probably wouldn't be able to get a signal anyway, but I wasn't sure what else to do.

I raced all the way to the Butterfly Garden, but there was no sign of Rosa May either. She wasn't on the bridge or lying in our usual shady spot under the trees. The Garden felt empty without her. What if she was still angry? What if she'd been serious when she said she wasn't going to bother showing up? If only I could take back what I'd said when we rowed. Tears pricked the corners of my eyes. I really needed to see her.

I picked out a tiny pink butterfly while I was waiting and began to follow it around. It was one of our favourite games, but it felt lonely playing it by myself. The butterfly settled on a flower for a few moments and then took off across the field. I rushed after it, pretending it was magic and that it would lead me straight to Rosa May. *The*

Garden is full of magic butterflies, she was always saying, *you just have to know how to spot them.*

I followed the butterfly down to the lake. It hovered around the edge for a bit, flitting from flower to flower, before flying straight across the middle. I dashed onto the bridge as fast as I could, and over to the other side, but there was no sign of it. I ran one way and then another and was on the verge of giving up when it appeared suddenly from behind a tree.

"You're back," I cried, wishing it was Rosa May, desperate to see her, but just then an identical pink butterfly flew out from behind the same tree and it was impossible to tell them apart.

I collapsed down in the grass and watched the butterfly twins chase each other around. I wondered what Mack was doing right that minute. My face grew warm thinking about the way he'd held me in the water; how embarrassing it felt to be that close to him, even if it was only a swimming lesson. The two pink butterflies flew over my head. I swivelled round, trying to keep my eye fixed on one without getting it confused with the other, when I noticed a woman on the other side of the lake. There were quite a few people around that morning and she had her back to me, but there was something about her that caught my attention.

She was dressed all wrong for a start. She had a heavy coat wrapped around her, as if it was the middle of winter, and she was wearing short, furry boots. I recognized the coat and the boots straight away. I'd seen them a hundred times. I shrank back into the grass, holding my breath as she turned round and stared straight out across the lake. It was Mum.

I crouched down, making myself as small as possible. I had no idea what she was doing there, but I didn't want her to see me. It was impossible to make out her face from so far away, but for some reason I was sure she was crying. She was bent over slightly, and every now and then she swept her hand across her eyes.

I crept backwards, inching my way through the grass, watching her the whole time. What if she was sleepwalking? What if she wandered straight into the lake? I had to stop myself from calling out. What was she *doing* here? It was awful the way she was hunched over like that in her big winter coat. I wanted to go to her, to help her, but I didn't want her to know I'd been coming to the Garden. My body felt heavy, weighed down. I didn't know what to do.

I was still creeping back, just watching her, when someone grabbed me from behind. I whipped round, scared out of my wits, but it was only Rosa May.

"Don't do that," I hissed. "You nearly gave me heart failure!"

"I nearly gave *you* heart failure? What on earth are you doing?"

I pulled her down next to me, my heart beating so fast I could barely speak.

"What's the matter, Becky? You look as if you've seen a ghost."

"It's my mum. Over there on the other side of the lake. But I don't want her to see me."

Rosa May looked out across the water. She didn't say anything for ages, she just stared.

"I know she looks strange," I said, a bit embarrassed. "I don't know why she's wearing that coat when it's so hot."

"What's she doing here?"

"I'm not sure. She left the house before I got up. She's been acting really weird lately, especially since she left her job."

Rosa May dragged her eyes away from Mum. "Have you told her about coming here? Does she know we meet every day?"

I shook my head, still trying to catch my breath.

She grabbed my hand, squeezing it tight. "Is that why you didn't come yesterday?" she said urgently. "Because of your mum?"

I didn't know what to say. If I told her I'd been swimming with Mack, she wouldn't understand. She'd asked me to go swimming with her so many times – she'd literally begged me – but some of the things she did when she was messing about in the lake scared me half to death. The last thing I wanted to do was lie to her, but I couldn't face telling her the truth either.

"She's leaving, look." Rosa May nudged me, pointing at Mum. "Come on, let's go down to the bell heather and see if we can spot the Silver-studded Blue."

She pulled me up and we ran across the meadow, our hands laced together. I looked back a few times, but Mum had disappeared.

The rest of the morning dragged by. Rosa May was hyped up and restless. She wanted to play a new game, but I wasn't in the mood. It involved trapping a butterfly with our bare hands and then awarding each other points based on how rare it was.

"I'm not playing that," I said. "It's cruel. Why would you want to catch a butterfly anyway? Let's take some photos instead. We could try to get some really good close-up shots..."

Rosa May rolled her eyes, groaning. "Not photos again! That's all you ever want to do. It's *sooo* boring."

"Well, what's so exciting about catching a poor,

defenceless butterfly? What are you going to do with it once you've caught it?"

"Let it go of course," she said, tossing her hair over her shoulder. Challenging me to argue. "Why are you being such a killjoy? You might as well go home."

I went along with it in the end. I didn't want to, but I was tired and she dragged me into the game while I was still saying no. I hated the idea of trapping something so fragile, but Rosa May set about catching a butterfly as if her life depended on it. It seemed to take for ever but eventually she crept up behind a big yellow and black Swallowtail, closing her hands around it as it settled on a flower for some nectar.

The butterfly went crazy, beating its wings in terror, frantically trying to break free. The noise was awful.

"Stop it!" I cried. "Let it go!" I grabbed hold of her hands, forcing them open.

"What are you doing?" yelled Rosa May. "You've spoiled the game. It's not like I was going to hurt it."

"I don't care. It's horrible. I'm not playing any more."

Rosa May laughed, her eyes wild. "Suit yourself," she said, and skipped off, hands cupped together, ready to try again.

I lay in the grass, watching her. I'd never seen her so manic. It reminded me of this boy, Martin, at primary school, who used to have these sudden blowout rages. *It's as if you've got the very devil in you, Martin*, our teacher would say, and she'd wrap her arms around him and hold him tight until he calmed down.

She raced round and round the field, stalking every butterfly in sight, until she exhausted herself.

"You were right, this game's rubbish," she said in the end, flopping down next to me. She was lying so close I could hear her heart beating hard, like the wings of the trapped butterfly.

"I really think my mum's losing it, you know," I said after a bit. "She was so keen to come back and live in Oakbridge. She kept going on about making a fresh start and how great it would be to live in the country – but I swear she's cracking up."

"Are you going to ask her what she was doing here today?"

"No, of course not." I sat up, clasping my arms round my knees. "If she finds out I was here, she'll never let me come back."

Rosa May snorted. "Why not? She lets you go off by yourself every day anyway, so what's the difference? She doesn't seem that bothered about you at all."

I opened my mouth and shut it again. I didn't want to tell her. Not about the lake. If she found out Mum was terrified of the water and that neither of us could swim, she might insist on teaching me herself. Swimming was as natural to Rosa May as breathing, but the thought of going anywhere near the lake with her filled me with dread. Swimming with Mack in a pool was hard enough, but swimming with Rosa May in the lake was beyond scary.

"You still haven't told me where you were yesterday," she said suddenly, as if she could see right inside my head. "I asked you before but you didn't answer."

It was so hot. I began to feel strange. Rosa May was staring at me, waiting for me to say something.

"I've got to...to...get back," I stammered. "I've got to make sure my mum's okay." I felt dizzy suddenly. I put my head between my knees. "She's wandering around in her winter coat. I'm worried about her." I started to get up, but Rosa May grabbed me and pulled me back down.

"Just tell me, Becky. Where were you?" She squeezed my wrist.

"Don't do that, it hurts." I tried to yank my hand away but her grip was too strong. Our eyes locked for a second, both of us breathing hard, and then she let go, her face crumbling.

"I'm sorry," she cried. "It's just I was waiting and

waiting and you didn't come. I got here really early and I waited all day."

"It's okay. It's all my fault. I should've let you know. Don't get upset, Rosa May, please."

I was still finding it difficult to catch my breath. The air around us was thick and sticky like syrup. I helped her up and we stood there hugging for a second.

"I was lonely without you here," she whispered. "Don't ever let anyone come between us, Becky."

I shook my head, holding her tight. "I won't, I promise."

"On your life?"

I nodded. "On my life."

She walked me to the exit. It was still quite early, but I had to make sure Mum was okay. "I wish I could stay," I said, hugging her again.

She pulled back suddenly, her eyes searching my face. "Do you ever think about the end of the summer? About what's going to happen when school starts? And the weather changes? And the Garden closes for winter?"

I shook my head. "I don't want to think about it, it's too awful."

"But do you think we'll still be friends?"

"Of course we will!" I cried. "We'll always be friends. We'll meet up every weekend and after school, and when my mum's feeling better you can come and sleep over at mine."

"It won't be the same though, will it? It won't be the same as meeting up here every day." She paused for a moment. "Not unless I could find a way..."

"What are you talking about? Find a way to do what?"

She stared off over my shoulder, her eyes focused on something far away in the distance.

"A way to make the summer last for ever."

Chapter Fourteen

S he vanished back into the Garden before I could ask her what she meant. She was obviously hatching some plan, but it was never going to happen. Mum had enrolled me at the high school in Farnsbury before we'd even moved. It was supposed to be really good, miles better than my old school, but I was still dreading it. I'd found it hard enough when I started Year Seven and *everyone* was new – this time I'd be the *only* new girl.

Mum was already home when I got in. She was sitting at the table in her nightie, doing the puzzle. I was so relieved to see her, I rushed over and hugged her tight. She was still wearing her furry boots, but when I asked her why, she looked down, surprised, as if she hadn't even noticed she had them on.

I made her a cup of tea and we chatted for a bit, just about the weather and the washing-up. She was trying to fit a tiny piece of red into the field of poppies, but her hand was trembling slightly and she couldn't quite work out where it should go.

"I don't know why Stella bought me such a difficult puzzle," she said, tapping the tiny piece on the table over and over, until I reached across and took it away from her.

"I'll just make a start on the dishes," I said, "and then why don't we sit down together with the paper and have a look through the jobs section?"

Mum shrugged. "I've already looked, Becky. There's nothing in there. Nothing." She glanced up at me for a second, but her eyes were flat, as if someone had switched the lights off.

I got up anyway and put on Mum's apron. It was red and white with a frill round the edge and way too big. It was difficult to know where to start. The kitchen hadn't been cleaned properly for days and it was a state. I moved a pile of plates to one side to make some space by the sink and noticed a big white envelope tucked behind the toaster.

"What's this?" I asked, holding it up to show her.

Mum turned round. "No idea," she said vaguely. "It must've arrived earlier while I was out." She turned back, blushing suddenly, as if she'd just realized she was still in her nightie and that I wasn't supposed to know she'd been out in the first place.

Inside the envelope there was an invitation to little Albert's christening. It was printed on thick, cream card with two tiny blue feet in the middle and a silky blue ribbon at the top. I read it out to Mum.

"Julie and Robin would love you to attend the christening of their son, Albert Jonathan Jackson." Robin was Mr. and Mrs. Jackson's son. He lived about half an hour away but they'd decided to have the christening at Oakbridge church.

"I'm not going," said Mum, when I'd finished reading out all the details. She was animated suddenly, her eyes flashing.

"But we've *got* to. Mr. and Mrs. Jackson will be really upset. It's their first grandchild, and they're so excited."

"I don't care. I don't even know Julie and Robin, I've only met them once. Why can't people just leave me alone?"

"What do you mean?"

She was getting worked up, clenching and unclenching

her fists. "That's why I left in the first place. Everyone staring. Everyone *knowing*. How was I supposed to carry on?"

"Everyone knowing what? You're not making any sense. *Please*, Mum, everyone knowing *what*?"

She breathed in deeply, closing her eyes. "I'm sorry, Becky, really I'm so sorry. I only meant everyone knowing my business, that's all – but I'm not going to the christening, I really don't want to, and that's that."

I knew she wouldn't change her mind either. She was as stubborn as Rosa May when she wanted to be. I turned back to the sink to start the washing-up. It was getting harder and harder to imagine how Mum was going to sort herself out. She'd been low before – there were times in our old house when she'd moped about in her dressing gown for a few days, or put herself to bed for the weekend with a migraine – but I'd never seen her as bad as this.

I wasn't sure whether to leave her by herself the next morning. I was scared she might wander off again, or do something stupid – she was so out of it. I was still in the kitchen, deciding what to do, when Stella turned up.

"Mum's still in bed," I said, letting her in. "She's been acting really weird, especially in the last day or so. Not just sleeping a lot, other stuff as well. She said something yesterday about everyone staring at her, as if she's too scared to go out. I honestly don't know what to do any more."

Stella pulled me into her arms and gave me an enormous hug. "Don't worry, Becky, my love. We'll soon have her back on her feet. Your mum and I have helped each other through some pretty sticky times in the past, you know."

It was so nice to have a cuddle. I snuggled in even closer, breathing in her lovely sunny smell. "Can I just ask you something, Stella? What did you mean the other day, when you were talking to Mum and you said that I had a right to know? I heard you, as I was coming in."

She sighed heavily, shaking her head. Then she pulled away, holding me by the shoulders. "I'm really sorry, Becky, but it's not for me to tell you that. You'll have to ask your mum when she's feeling a bit stronger."

"But it's so frustrating. She won't tell me anything about my dad, or her life before she left Oakbridge. You don't know what it's like."

"I can't even imagine how hard it must be for you, but it's really got to come from her..."

"But..."

She held her hand up. "No more buts! Come on, we've got work to do." She grabbed a few things out of the fridge and somehow rustled up an omelette and toast and some freshly squeezed orange juice, laying it all out nicely on a tray. "It's so much better to tackle things on a full stomach," she said, winking at me. "That's what I always say to my Mack – not that he needs much encouragement."

It was weird hearing her talk about Mack. I couldn't stop thinking about the other day, wondering if he'd call. Wondering what he meant when he said we had *all summer*.

"Are you coming up then?" said Stella, heading for the stairs.

I shook my head. I didn't want to hang about to see if Mum was up to *tackling things*, as Stella put it. As soon as she disappeared up the stairs, I slipped out to see Rosa May.

Nothing much happened over the weekend. Rosa May wouldn't say anything else about her big plan to make the summer last for ever, just that she was working on it. We didn't spot the Silver-studded Blue, but neither did anyone else. Stella came by a lot. She did some shopping, and cooked us some proper meals, singing along to the radio at the top of her voice. And Mum spent most of the time in bed, sleeping, but Stella said that was okay, that she needed to build up her strength.

I loved it when Stella was there, busy in the kitchen, dancing around as if she was at a disco. It was the only time the house felt like a proper home. I was dying to know if Mack had told her we'd been swimming together. I nearly blurted it out a couple of times but I was worried she might discuss it with Mum.

I must've checked my phone about five hundred times an hour, hoping that he'd text me. I replayed our afternoon at the pool over and over, analyzing every word, every look, trying to work out if he liked me, or if he'd only suggested we hang out because Stella had asked him to.

On Sunday night they announced a hosepipe ban on the news. No one was allowed to water their gardens or wash their cars using a hosepipe until further notice. Forty-three days had passed since it last rained. It was so hot the motorways were beginning to melt. Mr. Jackson said it was all our own fault for making such a whacking great hole in the ozone layer.

"That's what's done it," he said on Monday morning, as I wandered by on my way to meet Rosa May. "We've only ourselves to blame for not looking after God's planet the way He intended. It's the likes of our Albert I worry about. What sort of state is the world going to be in when he grows up?"

I thought about my dad, out there somewhere, trying to look after the environment. I could just imagine him up in the sky, fixing the hole in the ozone layer with a giant plaster, or maybe sewing it back together with a supersized needle and thread. I asked Mr. Jackson if he believed the hole would ever shrink or disappear, but he shook his head as if it was far too late to put things right.

I didn't hear from Mack until later that day. He'd spent the weekend with his dad, at some out-of-town racing track, and he wanted to know if I'd go swimming with him the following morning. I said yes without thinking. I was going to suggest we do something else, *anything* else, but I was so excited he'd called, the words were out of my mouth before I could stop them. I still didn't really get why he was so keen to hang out with me. Maybe Rosa May was right and he was just bored because it was the summer holidays and there was nothing much else going on.

We arranged to meet outside the Jacksons' at ten. "I haven't forgotten what you promised last time," he teased, just before we said bye. "About putting your feet down."

My tummy tightened. "That was last time," I muttered. "I'm not promising anything."

I talked non-stop all the way to Farnsbury. I think it was nerves. Not just about swimming, but the fact that we were going by ourselves this time – it somehow felt more like a date. I told him about the wildlife photography course I'd done at my old school, and how I'd been spending loads of time at the Butterfly Garden.

"It's such a beautiful place! I've been able to take some great shots and my friend Rosa May and I have been searching for a very rare butterfly called the Silver-studded Blue. She's a brilliant swimmer actually," I babbled on. "She does all these crazy stunts in the water but they scare me half to death." I didn't know what I'd do if we actually bumped into Rosa May. She'd be so upset that I was seeing Mack behind her back, *and* going swimming with him.

"You'll be doing stunts soon," said Mack. "You're my star pupil, don't forget!"

"Your *only* pupil," I reminded him, laughing. "And I will *not* be doing any stunts!"

The leisure centre still felt familiar, but not quite in the same eerie way as it had the other day. The smell was just as bad and the noise was deafening but I suppose I was more prepared. I stood in the reception area, looking around, searching for clues – anything that might explain why I was so sure I'd been there before. The trouble was, it was just a feeling, not a proper memory that I could catch hold of.

Mack didn't waste any time chatting, or showing off his brilliant butterfly stroke like last time. It was straight down to business. As soon as we were changed and sitting on the side of the pool, he jumped into the water and then turned back towards me, clasping me under the arms and lowering me in with him, so I was clinging onto him with my legs around his waist like before.

It was cold and scary and I had to stop myself from squealing like a baby. I started to tremble all over, but I wasn't sure if that was because I was in the water, or in Mack's arms.

"Don't let go," I said, my teeth chattering. "I *am* going to put my feet down but you've got to swear you won't let go of me straight away."

"I swear," said Mack seriously. "I'd cross my heart, but if I did I might drop you!"

We stood there bouncing for a bit longer and then screwing up all my courage, I took the deepest breath and uncurled my legs from around Mack's middle. It was the strangest feeling, like being in space. My legs floated up and I had to push them down against the water, feeling for the bottom of the pool with my feet. Very slowly, I released my grip on Mack's shoulders.

"Look, Mack, I'm standing," I gasped. "I can't believe it. I'm actually standing up on my own in a swimming pool."

The bottom of the pool felt solid and safe. Not how I'd imagined it at all. Mack smiled and held my hands, and we faced each other, bouncing slightly.

"Now for lesson number two," he said, grinning.

"What do you mean? This *is* lesson number two."

He shook his head. "Uh-uh. Standing on your own was the end of lesson number one. Lesson number two involves bunny hops."

"*What?*"

"Bunny hops," he repeated. "We're going to bunny hop across the middle of the pool and back again."

"No way. I don't want to. I'm getting out." I turned towards the steps, trying to drag Mack with me.

"Hey, calm down, Becky. We'll get out in a minute, but first of all we're going to hop. It's not proper swimming, it's just hopping. Like a rabbit."

"*Like a rabbit?* R-r-rabbits don't even like water," I stuttered, my teeth beginning to chatter again.

But Mack wasn't listening. He was pulling me towards him, hopping backwards so that I had to hop forwards if I wanted to keep hold of his hands. We went all the way across to the other side and then Mack turned me round and we came back, bouncing along like a couple of bunnies. I concentrated very hard, holding onto his hands as tightly as I could, especially in the middle when the sides seemed a million miles away.

"How impressive is this?" cried Mack. "A week ago you'd never set foot in a pool and now look at you. You'll be swimming the Channel next."

"*Me?* Swimming the Channel?"

"Well, maybe not *swimming* it, but you could always try hopping across. They'll make a programme about it: *Becky Hops the Channel.* You'll be famous!"

"I don't want to be famous," I said, laughing. "Not for hopping, at any rate!"

We'd just about got back to where we started when Mack let go of one of my hands to wave at someone walking along the side of the pool towards us. I grabbed hold of him, terrified he was about to swim off.

"Don't panic, it's just my dad." As the man got closer, I could see he was tall and broad with very short brown hair. He was wearing a blue tracksuit and a blue and red baseball cap.

"This is Becky," said Mack. "I'm teaching her to swim. Becky, this is my dad, Colin."

Colin crouched down by the side of the pool. "Hello, Becky," he said. "It's nice to see you again after all these years."

"W-w-hat do you mean?" I stammered. "I've never met you before in my life."

"Of course you have," he laughed.

I froze, still holding onto Mack. It was as if all the noise had been sucked from the air, until the only sound I could hear was my heart slamming against my ribs.

"In fact the last time I saw you, you were right here, in this pool, clinging onto your dad and looking just about as scared as you do now!"

Chapter Fifteen

It was lucky Mack was holding me because everything started to spin.

"I haven't got a dad," I whispered. "I've never met him. You must be mixing me up with someone else."

Colin looked confused. He shook his head, rubbing his chin. "It was a long time ago, Becky. You were only a toddler..."

"It. Wasn't. Me," I repeated very slowly, as if he was stupid. But somewhere deep inside I think I knew it *was* me. It didn't make sense, but then nor had anything else since I'd arrived in Oakbridge.

Mack seemed just as confused as his dad. He lifted me

out of the pool and I sat on the side in a puddle of cold water, my arms wrapped around my knees.

"I've g-got to g-go," I said. "I've g-got to g-go straight home." My teeth were chattering so badly I could hardly speak.

Mack pulled himself out of the water and hurried round the pool to get my towel. Colin followed him and when he caught up they stood there talking, their heads close together. I watched them from where I was sitting. Mack shifted from one foot to the other, shrugging with his palms up. He glanced back at me and shrugged again. They talked for another minute and then Colin strode off, disappearing into an office at the side of the pool, through a door that said *Staff Only*.

I don't know how I managed to get changed. I was shaking all over and I couldn't make my arms and legs work properly to get my clothes on. How could Colin know me? How could he have seen me with my dad? It had to be a mistake – either that or Mum had lied to me about *everything*. I'd spent most of my life trying to find out why my dad wasn't around, but it felt much safer, suddenly, to imagine he'd been off in the rainforest fixing the planet, rather than right here at Farnsbury leisure centre.

"What was all that about?" said Mack when I came out to the front. "Are you okay?"

I nodded. "It's just that my mum left Oakbridge before I was born. That's what she's always told me – that I never met my dad – but now I'm not so sure."

"Well, my dad says he's certain he remembers you when you were a little girl, but he refused to say anything else. He didn't mean to upset you, Becky."

"I know, it's not his fault. I just need to talk to my mum."

We wandered down the road to the bus stop. "What are you going to do?" said Mack. "Are you going to tell her what he said?"

"I really want to, but it's complicated. My mum's been in such a state since she walked out on her job, and there's other stuff..." I hesitated, biting my lip. Mack was so easy to talk to, but I didn't want to pour out my entire life history. We were supposed to be having a laugh, but it had all turned so heavy.

"Well, I definitely think you should tell her," said Mack quietly. "When my mum and dad broke up they tried to hide things from me because they thought it would be for the best, that I wouldn't notice what was going on, but I just ended up thinking it was all my fault and that they were splitting up because of me."

"But why would my mum say she left Oakbridge when she was pregnant with me if she didn't? Why would she lie about that?"

"I don't have a clue," said Mack, "but whatever the reason, it's always better to know the truth."

I repeated that one line to myself all the way back to Oakbridge. *It's always better to know the truth. It's always better to know the truth.* I said it so many times it stopped making sense – it was just a string of random words. Mack chatted away, telling me all about his mum and dad getting divorced – about how Colin used to stay out late every night and see other women and about how he owed money to loads of different people – but it was impossible to concentrate. I knew I had to ask Mum the truth, but it suddenly seemed as if the truth might be so totally unbelievable, it would be like walking through a door into a completely different world.

I left Mack outside the Jacksons' and ran down to the Butterfly Garden to try and clear my head before I went home. I remembered what Rosa May had said when I told her about finding the photo – that if Mum had managed to keep a baby secret for so many years she might be keeping all sorts of other secrets from me too. She was waiting for me at our special shady spot, holding a long daisy chain.

"Look what I made for you, Becky," she called out as I ran towards her. "It took me ages and ages. It kept breaking." She jumped up to fasten the chain around my neck. I could feel her breath in my hair. It was such a relief to see her.

"How's your mum today? Is that why you're so late?"

I nodded, turning round to give her a hug. "She's worse than ever. And you were right, she's hiding all sorts of stuff from me. Stuff that happened years ago when I was a little girl." I had to be careful. I couldn't tell her about Colin or she'd know I'd been swimming with Mack. I hated keeping it from her, but I couldn't face another scene.

"You haven't told her about finding the photo have you?"

I shook my head. "No, I haven't said anything. Not yet."

"What do you mean, '*not yet*'? Are you planning to ask her about it then?"

"Not about the photo, not while she's in such a fragile state, but I do want to know about my dad." I blinked back tears. It was beginning to sink in. Colin had actually *seen* me with my dad. If he was right, if he really had seen us together at the pool, then my dad must've left *after* I was born, not before. And suddenly it came to me, flashing in front of my eyes like a massive neon sign: Mr. Jackson's crossword clue from all those weeks ago. *To cast away, leave or desert*, seven letters, first letter A. It was

Abandon. A needle of pain pierced deep into my heart. My dad had abandoned me.

I thought about how I'd scratched my name into the window sill the night before we moved, *just in case*. The *real* reason I'd been so desperate to leave my mark. Clinging to the hope that he was out there, searching for me, when he'd probably known where I was all along.

Rosa May was stroking my hair. "Does your mum ever talk about the past at all?" she said. "Has she told you *anything* about her old life in Oakbridge?"

"Not really," I said, feeling shaky. "I mean, I know she met my dad here when she was really young and that she was best friends with Stella, but that's it." I stood there in Rosa May's arms, feeling weak, as if my muscles had turned to water. I didn't know if it was the shock or the heat or both of them combined. I just wanted to lie down in the grass and go to sleep until everything was back to normal.

"I *hate* your mum," said Rosa May suddenly, spitting the words out like bullets.

I pulled away shocked. "What do you mean? You don't even know her."

She turned scarlet, her face burning up. I think it was the first time I'd ever seen her embarrassed. "I know enough," she said. "It's a small village, Becky. People talk."

"What people? What do you mean?"

"Just people," she muttered, and then jumped up before I could ask her what she was talking about. "I'm going for a swim if you want to join me," she called over her shoulder. But I shook my head, more confused than ever. Rosa May was the closest friend I'd ever had, but sometimes it felt as if I didn't know her at all.

I left the Garden while she was still swimming. I knew she'd be upset, but I was determined to talk to Mum and I had to get home before I lost my nerve. I'd asked her about my dad so many times, but I wasn't going to let her wriggle out of the conversation or twist things round this time. I'd tell her what Colin said, and then, when she was feeling stronger, I'd tell her I'd seen the photo. I needed to know about the past, about what happened before I was born; however difficult it was.

Mrs. Jackson was standing in the doorway of the shop, holding a baby in her arms.

"Come and meet our Albert," she called out. "He's five months old today!" Albert blew a raspberry and buried his face in Mrs. Jackson's shoulder.

"Oh, he's so sweet," I cried, reaching up to stroke his head. It was smooth and soft, like velvet. "Thank you for the invitation to the christening. I'll definitely be there, and hopefully Mum too."

Her face broke into a smile. "Oh, that's lovely. At least it'll be cool in the church, eh." She shifted Albert round so he was facing me. "Are you feeling okay, Becky? You're ever so pale."

"I'm fine, I'm just a bit tired," I said, anxious to get home. I tickled Albert under the chin and he reached for my finger, squeezing it tight.

"He's got a grip of iron for such a little thing," said Mrs. Jackson. "How's your mum getting on, by the way? Has she had any luck finding a job?"

"No, not yet, there doesn't seem to be much around. I should be getting back to her, to be honest. She's not feeling too good at the moment."

Mrs. Jackson nodded sympathetically. "Send her my best, won't you?"

Mum was sitting in her usual place, sorting out the green section of the puzzle. She'd finished the poppies over the weekend and had moved onto the fields.

"Look at this," she said, as I came in. "It's impossible. I'm trying to separate the pieces but they're almost identical. I never realized there were so many similar shades of green."

"Mack's dad Colin said he's met me before. When I

was a little girl." My hands flew up to my mouth but it was too late. The words were out.

"I'm trying to do the dark green first," said Mum, as if I hadn't spoken. She didn't even turn round. "I don't think you understand quite how tricky it is."

"Are you listening to me, Mum? Stop going on about the stupid puzzle, can't you? Did you hear what I said? About Colin?"

"I could tell you some things about Colin," said Mum, pressing her fingers to the sides of her head. "He's not to be trusted. He's a terrible liar. Leaving him was the best thing Stella ever did."

"*Mum*, I don't care about Colin and Stella and their marriage. Colin said the last time he saw me at the pool I was *with my dad*."

"What do you mean, the *last time* he saw you at the pool?" She whipped round to face me, her eyes blazing. "Tell me you haven't been at the pool, Becky! Why were you there? You haven't been *swimming*, have you?"

She was doing it again. Her usual trick. "Stop it! Stop twisting things round. So what if I've been swimming? He *says* I was a toddler. And that I was *with my dad*. My dad, who according to you *I've never met*!" I was shouting now, waving my arms about. "Why have you lied to me? You've lied about everything! You said he left before I was born!"

Mum's face was bright red. She pulled at her top as if it was too tight round her neck. "Becky, I..." She slumped forward suddenly, holding her head in her hands. I should've stopped. I should've realized she couldn't cope, but I was keyed up and angry and desperate to know the truth.

"And that's not all!" I screamed, running out of the room. I tore up the stairs, unable to stop now I'd started. I crawled under Mum's bed, reaching for the box. "I *know*!" I yelled, as I flew back down the stairs. "I know about the photo!"

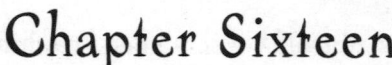

Chapter Sixteen

I raced back into the kitchen, holding the box out in front of me, ready to bring everything into the open. But Mum wasn't sitting at the table any more; she was lying collapsed in a heap in the middle of the floor. And she wasn't moving.

I dropped the box and ran to her side, grabbing a tea towel to put under her head. Her body was in a funny position, twisted up, with her legs jutting out at a weird angle.

"Wake up, Mum, come on, *please* wake up." I grasped hold of her shoulders to give her a shake but she was too heavy. "*MUM!*" I shouted in her ear but she didn't even flinch. I tried to remember what you're supposed to do when someone collapses. We did this first-aid thing at school once, about airways and breathing, but I couldn't get it straight in my head. I shook her again. Her face was horribly red and puffy. "Wake up, Mum, wake up. Just *please*, wake up."

She groaned slightly and her eyelids fluttered. I leaped up and ran out to the hall to call an ambulance.

"My mum's collapsed," I said as soon as someone answered, and then I burst out crying. I don't know how I got out the address or gave any proper details, I was sobbing so hard. The woman kept telling me to take deep breaths, and she stayed on the phone until the ambulance arrived, talking in this slow, calm voice. She asked me my name and if I was alone with Mum and if there was anyone they could call, but I couldn't work out the answers.

Everything happened very fast after that. The ambulance men rushed in, put an oxygen mask over Mum's face and then lifted her onto a stretcher, asking me loads of questions at the same time: her name, her age, what she'd eaten, if she'd been drinking, or taking any medication. The questions went on and on as we climbed into the back of the ambulance.

I tried to explain that it was all my fault. That I'd found a box under her bed and it was supposed to be a secret and that I'd asked her about my dad. I said a whole load of other stuff about swimming and Mack and lying to Mum. The words came tumbling out, mixed up and confused. I couldn't stop. There was a nurse in the back. She told me her name was Pam and she put a heavy blanket round me and cuddled me close.

"You've had a nasty shock, Becky," she said, stroking my hair. "Everything's going to be okay now, you'll see."

As soon as we got to the hospital, they whisked Mum away on a trolley. I tried to follow but Pam pulled me back – she said I had to stay with her until Mum was sorted. She led me into the main waiting area and handed me a cup of sweet tea. It was in one of those polystyrene cups and burning hot. "Have a few sips of this, the sugar will help with the shock, and then we'll see about getting someone to look after you." She kneeled down in front of me. "Do you have a number for your dad, Becky? Is he at work?"

I shook my head. "My mum looks after me. It's just me and Mum. It's *always* been me and Mum."

Pam stood up, sighing. "Okay, my love. I'm just going to pop over to the desk for a minute and make a few phone calls."

I sat there, trembling all over. I couldn't believe I'd been so stupid. I should've listened to Rosa May. She was right all along. She said Mum wouldn't be able to cope.

Why hadn't I kept my mouth shut? I could see Pam at the reception desk. She was on the phone but she kept glancing over. I picked at the edges of the cup, wondering who she was talking to.

I was still sitting there when Stella came bursting through the doors. I don't know how they found her except I think I might have said something about her being Mum's friend when we were in the ambulance. I jumped up and ran into her arms. It was such a relief to see someone familiar.

"Where is she, Becky?" she said, holding me tight. "What happened?"

"It was all my fault," I sobbed. "I found this box under her bed and her head was hurting and—"

"Hey, come on, calm down. It is *not* your fault. I don't want to hear you say that." She cupped my face in her hands. "None of this is your fault, Becky. None of it. Do you understand?" I stared up at her, nodding. She wiped away my tears and gave me another hug. "I'll go and have a chat with Pam, tell her I'm here to look after you, and then we'll find out how Mum is, okay?"

We had to wait for ages for any news, but eventually the doctor came out to tell us that Mum was okay. He said she was very weak and that her blood pressure was sky-high, but that she'd soon be back on her feet.

"We're going to keep her in for a day or two and run some tests, but I'm not expecting to find anything too serious." He reached out and ruffled my hair. "I hear you're to be commended for your quick thinking, young lady – calling the ambulance and looking after your mum until it arrived. She's lucky to have a clever girl like you."

I just stared at him. I wasn't clever, I was stupid. Whatever Stella said, Mum had only collapsed because of me and my big mouth. I wasn't going to say another word. Not to Mum or Stella or the doctors. I wanted to know the truth more than ever, I was *desperate* to know, but there was no way I was going to confront Mum again.

"I'll be staying with Becky for a few days until her mum's up and about," Stella was saying to the doctor. "I've spoken to my ex-husband and he's happy to have my son until Tracy's well enough to come home."

The doctor glanced at Stella over my head. "Could we have a quick chat before you go? I just need to tie up some loose ends, if that's okay." They walked off to the side, their heads close together. Pam came over from the desk to wait with me.

"Can I see my mum now?" I asked in a small voice.

She smiled. "You can pop up for a second. But you mustn't wake her if she's sleeping."

Mum was sleeping. She was lying in a big metal bed,

attached to lots of wires and tubes. She looked small and fragile, like she could slip away at any moment and no one would even notice. I leaned over the bed to kiss her cheek but she didn't move.

"I'm sorry, Mum," I whispered. "I'm sorry I shouted at you and called you a liar. I didn't mean it." I turned round to Pam. "Are you sure she's okay? She's so still."

"She's fine," said Pam firmly. "Really. Let's get you home now, Becky, you'll be needing a rest too."

I smoothed Mum's hair off her face and kissed her cheek again. "I'll make it up to you, I promise. Just get better, *please*."

It was awful going back to the house with Stella. I was too scared to go in at first. I kept imagining Mum collapsed on the floor in the middle of the kitchen, lying in that horrid, twisted-up position. The first thing I did was put the box back under her bed. I didn't even look inside. I was sorry I'd ever found it in the first place.

Stella tried her best to be cheery and bright but it wasn't the same without Mum there. She bustled around the kitchen, making toast and tea, but just the smell of it made me feel ill. I tried to force some food down, but my throat was clogged up. If only I hadn't said anything. If only I'd sat down with Mum and helped her with the puzzle or done the washing-up, or...

"Come on, Becky, eat up, you've got to stay strong for your mum."

"I just keep thinking of her all alone in that big metal bed. What if she wakes up and I'm not there. She'll be worried about me. We've never been apart before. Not even for one night."

Stella reached for my hand across the table. "The nurses will tell her where you are, love; they're looking after her really well. I know it all seems bleak and hopeless tonight but everything will seem brighter in the morning. I'll nip back from work at lunchtime and take you up to see her, I promise."

I sat up in bed for ages that night, trying to work things out in my head; all the different pieces of the puzzle. Mum said it was the new job that brought her back to Oakbridge – that it was supposed to be this great opportunity – but why did she leave Oakbridge in the first place? Was it my dad? Did he do something to her? Is that what she meant about *everyone knowing*? And who *was* the baby in the photo? Something drove her away and something brought her back, and apart from Mum, there was only one other person who knew the whole story and that was my dad.

* * *

I woke up feeling groggy, like I was lost in a thick fog. I had the tightest knot in my stomach but it took me a few moments to remember why. Downstairs, the kitchen was sparkly clean and Stella had left me a note by the jigsaw puzzle saying she'd see me at midday. It was nearly ten already, but if I left straight away, I'd have just about enough time to get down to the Butterfly Garden to see Rosa May.

It was already warm out, but misty, as if the whole of Oakbridge was trying to keep secrets from me. I started off walking but as I got nearer to the Garden I felt scared suddenly and broke into a run. The knot in my stomach was worse, like something terrible was about to happen and there was nothing I could do to stop it. I swear I could hear Rosa May calling for me, but somehow the faster I ran, the longer it seemed to take.

I spotted her as soon as I arrived. She was lying face down in the middle of the lake, her arms and legs spread out in the shape of a star. I raced across the field, calling her name and waving my arms. She must've heard me coming because she started to swim towards the side, but then just before she reached me she disappeared under the water. She was showing off – or punishing me for leaving without saying goodbye the day before. I watched for her, my eyes fixed on the surface, counting in my head, holding my breath. I should've been used to her trying to scare me by now, but it got to me every time.

I scanned the lake, searching for some sign she was there, but it was completely still. *Come on, Rosa May, come on.* My phone buzzed suddenly, making me jump. It was a text from Mack: *I heard about your mum – r u ok?* I didn't know what to text back. I still wanted to see him, so much, but I felt weird after what had happened at the pool with Colin – really embarrassed.

"Hey!" It was Rosa May. "What are you doing?"

I switched off my phone and slipped it back in my pocket as she pulled herself out of the lake.

"My mum's in hospital," I gabbled, grabbing her arm. "I called her a liar. I tried to show her the photo but she collapsed. It was awful, Rosa May, she was just lying there on the floor in the middle of the kitchen. I was certain she was dead. I didn't tell the doctor, or Stella, but that's what I thought when I saw her."

My legs felt as if they were going to give way. I sank down into the grass, dizzy and short of breath. Rosa May stood over me. "Why the hell did you do that?" she spat. "I told you what would happen. Why didn't you listen to me?"

"I don't know," I said, shrinking back. "I just wanted to find out the truth. There are so many secrets. It's driving me mad."

"How is she now? Is she going to be okay?"

I nodded. "The doctor said he's running some tests but she should be coming home today or tomorrow at the latest. Stella stayed last night and she's taking me up to the hospital at twelve. I'll have to get going in a sec."

Rosa May looked stricken. "Don't go yet, you've only just got here." She sat down next to me in the grass. "Hey, you'll never guess what happened yesterday, after you left. There was this woman here with her two children and they said they'd spotted a Silver-studded Blue. It was the big news of the day. Everyone was talking about it."

"I don't believe you." My palms were clammy suddenly. I couldn't bear it if someone else had spotted the Silver-studded Blue first, not with Mum so ill in hospital. It was only an old wives' tale, a stupid myth, but I couldn't help feeling that if I was the first to spot the Silver-studded Blue this summer, then I'd know for sure that my dad was on his way home to see me. And I needed him now more than ever before.

"It's true," said Rosa May. "They took photos and everything. You should've seen Maggie and Jean, they were beside themselves with excitement! But in the end, after all the fuss, it wasn't a Silver-studded Blue at all, it was an *Adonis* Blue."

"How do you know?" My voice was shaking. "Did you see the photos? Are you sure?"

"Positive. The Adonis Blue is similar and it's really beautiful, but it's not that rare. I've seen loads."

"So you mean we still might find the *first* Silver-studded Blue?"

"We *are* going to find it first. I promised, didn't I?" She laced her fingers through mine, squeezing tight. "I never break my promises, Becky. You should know that by now."

We lay back in the grass together, gazing up at the sky. It was warm and peaceful and safe. Rosa May stroked my hair and murmured to me in a soft, hypnotic voice. I tried to sit up a few times but she pulled me back down into the grass. I was so tired after everything that had happened. There was so much I didn't understand. My eyes started to close. If I stayed right here, I might spot the first Silver-studded Blue, and then I'd know my dad was on his way home to put things right, to help my mum get better. I could feel my worries float away, melting into the early morning mist.

As I drifted off to sleep I thought I heard Rosa May say, "There's no need to go anywhere now, Becky. This is where you belong. Right here in the Butterfly Garden."

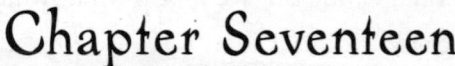

Chapter Seventeen

I woke up drenched in sweat. My mouth was dry and it was difficult to swallow. I knew without looking at my watch that I was late – I could tell by where the sun was in the sky. I dragged myself up. I had to get to the hospital to see Mum. I looked around for Rosa May, but she'd gone. I wish she'd woken me before she left, but she probably thought I needed the sleep after everything that had happened.

It seemed to take for ever to get back. Stella was outside the cottage, leaning against her car with her phone in her hand.

"Becky, where were you?" she called out. "I've left loads of messages – I was really worried."

I ran up to her. "I'm so sorry, Stella. My phone was turned off. It's not too late to go, is it? I really need to see Mum."

"No, it's fine. Come on, we'll pop up now and find out what's going on."

She got in the car and reached across to unlock the door on my side. "Why did you disappear like that, Becky? I know you're upset about your mum but I keep telling you, it's not your fault."

"It wasn't that. I just went to meet my friend to tell her what happened and we were lying in the grass talking and I dropped off to sleep. I was so tired, I hardly slept last night. Please don't be cross, Stella, I didn't mean to worry you."

She rolled her eyes, grinning. "Of course I'm not cross. I'm not in any great hurry to get back to work so you've done me a favour really."

We drove on for a bit in silence. I glanced at Stella. She was such a good friend to Mum and she'd been so lovely to me, but I knew at some point she'd have to go home to Mack. I wasn't joking when I'd said to Pam yesterday that it had only ever been me and Mum. Having Stella around, singing and dancing, cooking proper meals and cleaning up afterwards, normal stuff like that, made me realize just how lonely my life with Mum could be.

"I've been thinking about my dad," I blurted out suddenly. My mouth was so dry that the words felt sticky, as if they were coated in glue. "Do you think he'd ever look after me, if Mum was too weak to manage, or if she had to stay in hospital for a long time? He's a conservationist, you know," I added.

Stella smiled but she looked sad. "I know he is," she said. "And I know your mum doesn't like to talk about the old days, but he was a lovely man, your dad."

"Really?" I stared at Stella, amazed. "Do you mean that?" My eyes filled with tears. "I was sure he must've done something awful to Mum. Hurt her in some way, and that's why she left him."

"Not your dad," she said quietly. "He wouldn't hurt a fly. He was the sort of man who would take an injured bird home in a box and nurse it back to health."

"That's like me," I whispered. "I love animals too."

Stella nodded. "I know, sweetheart. You're just like him. In lots of ways."

I tried to take in what she was saying. I had so many questions, so much I wanted to ask her, but we'd arrived at the hospital.

"Does he still live in Oakbridge?" I said quickly. "Do

you know where he is? Do you ever see him?"

"No, my love, he left the village a long time ago, but if you want to know anything else you'll have to ask your mum; I've said far too much already."

Mum seemed so much better. She was sitting in a chair by her bed with a cup of tea, leafing through a magazine. Her eyes lit up as we came in and I rushed over to give her a hug.

"You look great," I said. "Have they told you when you can come home? Is your blood pressure down? You won't believe how clean the kitchen is – it's sparkling! But we haven't touched the puzzle, have we, Stella? We left that for you."

Stella laughed. "Don't bombard her, Becky. How are you, Trace? You gave us quite a scare."

"I'm feeling much better," said Mum. "To tell you the truth, I don't actually remember much about what happened, it's all a blur. I know I'd finished the poppies and that I was just about to make a start on the field, and then the next thing I remember is waking up here, wired up to all these machines."

"Are you serious?" I said. "You mean, you don't remember anything else?"

"Not at the moment, but the doctor said it might come back."

I kneeled down by the chair, resting my head on her lap while she chatted to Stella. I hoped her mind would stay blurred for ever. I didn't want her to remember a single word of what I'd said to her. The box was back under her bed and I was never going to mention it again. I was desperate to find out about my dad, especially after what Stella had said in the car, but I wasn't going to ask Mum, not while she was so ill. Rosa May was right. Some secrets were better off left alone.

We were only there for a bit when a nurse came bustling in and asked us to leave. I was sure they'd let her come home with us but they said they wanted to keep an eye on her for one more night, just in case. Mum got quite teary, clinging onto me and begging me not to leave her.

"Come on, Tracy," said Stella firmly. "You're upsetting Becky. We'll come and get you tomorrow. It's only a few more hours."

I gave her one last hug and ran out of the room before I started crying myself. I still felt as if I was to blame, whatever Stella said.

We went back up the next morning but it took ages to sort everything out. I started to wonder if they'd ever let her leave. She had to have her blood pressure checked again and then there were prescriptions to sort out and all these forms to sign.

"She needs lots and lots of rest," the doctor said, while Mum was in the other room with the nurse. "I'd like to see her back here at the beginning of next week, but any headaches and she's to come straight back in."

"Don't worry," I said. "I'm going to look after her. I'll do all the shopping and cooking and keep the house clean. She won't have to lift a finger."

"I'm sure you'll do a splendid job," he said, "but you're very young to be caring for your mum. Are there any other family members who might be able to help out...?" He paused, looking over my head at Stella.

"I'll be stopping by every day," she said quickly. "To look after Tracy *and* Becky. I'm as good as family, aren't I, Becky?"

I edged towards the door, nodding. "I'll just go and find Mum now," I said, anxious to leave. I didn't want him to think we couldn't manage.

The doctor bent his head close to Stella's. "I've also suggested to Tracy that she go to her GP and ask for some counselling and maybe some medication for depression," I heard him say quietly. "She's very low and I think it might be helpful for her to talk to someone."

A wave of frustration rolled over me. Mum might need to talk to someone but it was me she should be talking to, not a counsellor. I was so grateful to Stella for telling me about my dad, but I had even more questions now. If he was such a lovely, gentle man, why did he leave us? And why did Mum find it so difficult to talk about him? I couldn't ask her, not after today. I only wish she felt able to tell me herself.

I hardly left the house over the next few days. The furthest I went was down to the Jacksons' to buy milk and other bits and pieces we needed. Mrs. Jackson had heard about Mum being in hospital and she'd been busy cooking. The first day I dropped by, she'd made us some scones with home-made jam, and there was a delicious apple pie about to come out of the oven.

"I was baking anyway, what with the christening coming up, so a few more scones weren't going to make any difference." We were sitting in the kitchen behind the shop. It was small and hot and filled with the smell of buttery apples. The window sill was crammed with tomato plants and five jars of strawberry jam with pretty red and white checked cloths covering the lids.

"We heard the ambulance arrive," Mrs. Jackson went on, bending down to check on the pie. There was a sudden burst of heat as she opened the oven door and my eyes started to water. She peered at me anxiously. "You must've had an awful shock, Becky, seeing your mum like that. Are you sure you're okay? I know how hard it is when Mr. Jackson's poorly."

"I'm fine," I said. "Really. Mum's happy to be home and Stella's been helping out loads."

Mum *was* happy to be home, to begin with. She made an effort to stay up the first evening, and we had a nice supper together. She even promised to come to Albert's christening when Mrs. Jackson dropped the scones round. But by the next morning, her mood had plunged back down and it was a struggle to get her out of bed.

She spent most of the following few days sleeping, and when she did manage to get up, the only thing she seemed interested in was the puzzle. She'd sit at the table for hours, holding one tiny piece in her hand and moving it from place to place, trying to work out where it should go. She said it helped to take her mind off things, but I began to wonder if maybe the doctor at the hospital was right and she did need to see a proper counsellor.

Mack tried to get in touch a couple of times, but I couldn't face talking to him or going for any more swimming lessons. I didn't even go to the Butterfly Garden to see Rosa May. I was far too scared to leave Mum by herself. I knew Rosa May would be hurt; she wouldn't understand. I could almost hear her voice in my head demanding to know where I was, but there was nothing I could do.

The days dragged by. It was hot and stuffy. I was tense, churned up, waiting for something to happen. It was like Mum was there but not there; I don't think I'd ever felt so alone. At night, I sat in my airless room on my bed and wrote letters to my dad. I had no idea where he was or where I could send them, but I wrote them anyway. They were all slightly different, but the basic message was the same:

Dear Dad, it's me, Becky. I know you're off somewhere fixing the world, but please could you come home for a while and help me to fix my mum...

As the week went on, Mum seemed to shrink more and more inside herself. She was weighed down with sadness. I did everything I could to cheer her up, but it didn't make the slightest difference. I'd chat away, making plans, trying to involve her, but she'd stare right past me as if I wasn't there. I was just about to admit to Stella that I couldn't cope on my own any more – that I needed help – when the day for Albert's christening arrived.

And that's when everything changed for ever.

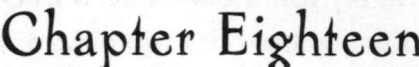

Chapter Eighteen

We'd been living in Oakbridge for exactly five weeks on the day of Albert's christening. I woke up early and lay in bed, thinking about Rosa May. I hadn't seen her for days, but the longer we were apart, the more I could hear her calling for me, as if we were attached by some sort of invisible thread and she was drawing me back to the Butterfly Garden.

It was already too warm in my room. I went into the bathroom and splashed cold water on my face. It helped, but only for a moment. They said the temperature was expected to reach over thirty-five degrees later on, the hottest day so far. Mum had promised she'd come to the christening when Mrs. Jackson dropped the scones round, but when I went in to wake her she wouldn't budge.

"I've got a splitting headache, Becky. It came on last night and it's killing me."

"You'll have to go back to the hospital if you've got a headache," I warned. "You know what the doctor said."

Mum slid further down the bed, groaning. "Not the hospital, *please*. I'll be fine in a bit. I just can't face the christening, that's all."

I didn't like to push it, not after last time. It didn't surprise me really. Mum's never been keen to go to church. She says she lost her faith years ago – but it's another one of those things she doesn't like to talk about.

The christening was due to start at eleven thirty, followed by lunch in the church hall. I had a shower and put on my nicest outfit: a dark purple sundress with matching purple pumps and the necklace Mum bought me that day she went shopping with Stella. There wasn't much time, but I decided to slip down to the Butterfly Garden before I set off for the church. I couldn't bear to let another day pass without seeing Rosa May.

"What a pretty dress," said Maggie, when I got to the Garden. "Are you off somewhere nice?"

"I'm going to a christening. It's for Mrs. Jackson's grandson, Albert."

"Oh, how lovely," said Maggie, clapping her hands together. "Well, you look a treat, you really do."

I smiled, thanking her, then ran straight through to the little shop and out into the Garden. Joan didn't bother stamping my hand any more. I think she just assumed I'd be coming and added me to her list of visitors.

It took me a while to find Rosa May. She wasn't on the bridge or in the lake. I thought I saw a flash of blue just beyond the bridge, but when I got across to the other side there was no sign of her. I sat down for a minute to catch my breath. It was unbearably hot and I could feel my dress sticking to me like melted toffee. I was just about to give up and go when suddenly she was there, wrapping her arms round my neck, laughing in delight. Maybe she'd been watching me all along.

"Finally!" she cried. "I've been waiting for ever!"

I jumped up to give her a hug. "I know. I'm sorry. My mum's been really ill. She's back from the hospital but I was scared to leave her on her own."

"But what about me? I've been on my own too. It's been awful. I'd almost given up hope." She stepped back from me, looking me up and down. "Why are you wearing that lovely dress? Where are you going?" Her eyes narrowed. "You're not meeting that boy Mack, are you?"

"No, of course not. I'm going to a christening. Hey, you don't want to come with me, do you?" I said, excited suddenly. "I'm sure Mrs. Jackson wouldn't mind. The invitation was for me and Mum but I couldn't get her out of bed this morning, and we'd have so much fun if we went together."

Rosa May snorted. "*What?* Go to church on a beautiful day like this? You've got to be joking!" She grabbed my hands, hyped up and jumpy. "Don't go either, Becky. You don't *have* to, do you? Why don't you stay here with me instead? They said it's going to reach nearly thirty-eight degrees today and the hotter it is, the more likely we are to spot the Silver-studded Blue."

I shook my head, sighing. "I can't. Mr. and Mrs. Jackson will be upset enough that Mum's not going."

Rosa May pushed me away suddenly. "Why did you bother coming here then?" she snapped. "You keep doing that. You turn up and then you leave straight away. Don't you want to be my friend any more, Becky? Is that it? Is that why I haven't seen you for days?"

"Don't say that! Of course not. I told you, it's my mum. I couldn't come because of my mum."

"But you're not worried about leaving her today, are you?" she sneered. "You're quite happy to go off to this christening or whatever it is. Don't you think you'd better stay at home if you're that concerned about her? I'm so sick of your stupid excuses!"

I wanted to explain, to put my point across, but I felt dizzy again, as if my head was filled with fluff. Every time I saw Rosa May lately, we ended up arguing. I didn't have the strength to fight with her any more.

"I am worried about my mum, but I didn't want to upset Mrs. Jackson. And I'm here, aren't I?" She didn't say anything. She was watching me. Waiting. "Look, I'll come tomorrow, first thing, and I'll stay all day. I promise."

"Cross your heart and hope to die?" she demanded, her eyes glittering. I'd never seen her this angry. It was like she couldn't bear it unless she had me all to herself.

I backed away, nodding. "Cross my heart and hope to die."

The church was packed. Mr. and Mrs. Jackson were standing at the doors, greeting people and guiding them to their seats. Mrs. Jackson looked lovely. She was wearing a pale pink dress with a matching hat, and she'd got Mr. Jackson into a suit.

"She's forced me to wear a tie," he said, winking at me. "In this heat! I'll be slipping it off as soon as the service starts."

"No you will not!" said Mrs. Jackson, wagging her finger at him. "Where's your mum, Becky? Couldn't she make it?"

"She's got a headache," I said. "She's really sorry."

"Not to worry. Pop yourself over there by Stella and Mack."

I looked across to where she was pointing. Stella was all glammed up in a bright multicoloured dress and a hat with a massive feather, but my eyes were drawn to Mack. I'd only ever seen him in shorts and a T-shirt, or in his swimming gear, but today he was wearing smart grey trousers and a white shirt with the sleeves rolled up. His arms were strong and tanned and the thought of him holding me in the pool made my face burn up. He turned round suddenly as if he could sense me watching, and waved me over.

"You look nice," he said, shifting up to make room. "Purple really suits you."

Stella laughed. "What a charmer! I don't know where he gets it from! How are you, Becky? How's Mum this morning?"

"Not so great," I said, tearing my eyes away from Mack. "She's got a headache again but she didn't want me to call the hospital. I think she might need to talk to someone." I looked down at my hands. "You know, someone, erm... professional."

Stella took hold of my hands and squeezed them.

"Don't worry, my love. She's got her follow-up appointment tomorrow afternoon. I'll take her up there and speak to the doctor myself. We'll soon get her sorted."

I wanted to ask her how we were going to do that – how we were ever going to get her sorted – but just at that moment Father Hill appeared at the front of the church and everyone stopped talking. The christening only lasted for about half an hour. There were some prayers and some singing and then Albert's mum and dad brought him up to the front. He was wearing this frilly white dress and Father Hill poured water on his head, blessing him in the name of the Father, the Son, and the Holy Spirit. Albert cried a bit and so did Mrs. Jackson, but you could tell she was chuffed to bits.

I liked Father Hill straight away. He was quite old, and even though he'd probably done a million christenings before, he put so much feeling into the service. He had this big, booming voice that echoed around the church, but there was something gentle about him, especially the way he was with Albert.

"He seems nice," I whispered to Stella. "Really kind. Maybe *he* could talk to Mum?"

Stella shook her head. "I think we'd be better off discussing it with the doctor. Especially if she's still getting headaches."

When the service was over we all trooped next door to the church hall for sandwiches, cake and tea. Father Hill was standing with Mrs. Wilson, greeting people as they came in. I wanted to talk to him, but not with Mrs. Wilson there. I only wanted to say that I'd enjoyed the service and that I might try to come the following Sunday, but she was giving me the evils again; staring at me as if I had three heads. I remembered what Mack said about her performing exorcisms and I shrank back, wondering why she always looked at me like that.

"Let's get some cake," said Mack, steering me away from Mrs. Wilson and towards the food. "Mrs. Jackson easily bakes the best scones in Oakbridge."

"I know, she brought some round this week."

We helped ourselves to scones and cake and found somewhere to sit. Neither of us said anything for a bit. It was the first time I'd seen him since that day at the pool and I could feel it hanging between us, making things awkward. I was dying for him to crack a joke, go back to the way he was before, but he was fidgety and restless.

"Look, I'm sorry about the other day," he said in the end, not quite meeting my eye. "You know, what my dad said and everything. I wish he'd kept his mouth shut, to be honest – I could see how much it shook you up."

"It's okay," I said, embarrassed. "He was only saying what he thought was true."

"Did you tell your mum in the end?"

I nodded, swallowing. "It was awful. I shouted at her. I called her a liar and then I ran out of the room to get something, this photo, and when I came back in to show her, she was on the floor, unconscious. That's why she ended up in hospital."

He leaned forward. "What was the photo of?" he asked.

I rubbed my hands on my dress. They were slick with sweat. I knew I could trust Mack, he was so nice, but I still found it difficult to say the words out loud. I breathed in deeply. "A baby. My mum in hospital with a baby. It was taken twelve years before I was born so I know it wasn't me – but I'm pretty sure it's a little girl because she's wrapped in a pink blanket. The thing is, my mum's never mentioned her."

"Wow." Mack opened his mouth and closed it again. "That's crazy, Becky. Are you sure it's her baby?"

I held out my hands, shrugging. "I don't know. I think so, but I don't know for sure." Suddenly, a thought that had been niggling away at the back of my mind popped into my head. "And that's not all. Ever since we've been back in Oakbridge, things have been really strange. Like, this note came through the door asking to meet me, it was weeks ago now. I thought it was from my dad but then your mum said he left Oakbridge years ago, so now I'm not sure who it was from or if it was even for me."

Mack sat for a minute, taking it all in. "Listen," he said slowly. "I know your mum's not well, but I really think you need to ask her about all of this. Show her the photo, and the note. Find out who the baby is. It might even explain why your dad left Oakbridge."

"I can't, Mack. You don't know what she's like. She's so secretive. And she's scared. What if she collapses again? I'd never forgive myself."

"I know it's risky, but seriously, Becky, you can't just pretend you never found it."

We were still talking when Mrs. Jackson came over with Albert. She was cradling him in her arms, showing him off to everyone. "Wasn't he a star?" she cried. "I thought I was going to burst with pride. Look at his little face! Isn't he a picture?"

"He's gorgeous," I said, stroking his hand. "It was a lovely christening, Mrs. Jackson, and the scones are delicious."

"Thank you, Becky, my love. I'm so pleased you could come. Have you met Father Hill?" She turned round just as Father Hill was making his way over to us.

"This is Becky Miller, Father. Tracy Miller's daughter," she said, introducing us.

"It's a pleasure to meet you, Becky," said Father Hill. He smiled warmly, as if he really meant it. "I hear your mum's been feeling poorly. I do hope she makes a speedy recovery. It must be so difficult for her, especially being back in Oakbridge after all this time. My heart goes out to her, it really does."

He moved on to greet someone else before I could say anything. Mack's eyes met mine. He grabbed me by the arm, blew kisses at Mrs. Jackson and Albert, and dragged me out of the hall.

"What on earth did he mean by that?" he hissed as soon as we were outside. "Why would it be difficult for your mum to be back in Oakbridge?"

"I don't know. I keep telling you, I don't know anything. She says she came back to Oakbridge because of this great new job she was offered, but that's rubbish. There's another reason, I'm sure of it."

"I asked *my* mum, you know," he said. I stared up at him, holding my breath. "After I got back from the pool that day. I asked her what my dad meant when he said he'd met you before, but she wouldn't tell me. She said it was up to your mum to tell you when she was ready."

I breathed out, disappointed. "Well, that's not about to happen any time soon, is it?"

We stood there in the blistering heat. I could tell Mack

was hatching a plan. I could almost hear him thinking.

"The photo," he said finally. "You need to look at the photo again when your mum's not there. See if there are any clues. Something you missed the first time you saw it."

I shook my head, frowning. "I can't. It's in a box under her bed. How am I supposed to get it? She spends practically every waking moment in her room these days! It's never going to happen."

"Yes it is," said Mack, clearly pleased with himself. "Tomorrow afternoon, when my mum takes her up to the hospital."

Chapter Nineteen

Mum was in the kitchen when I got in, working on the final section of the puzzle. She looked frail, her hair matted up from too much time spent in bed. Her movements were slow, unsteady, painful to watch. She didn't ask me about the christening. I'm not sure she even registered I was there. I sat down at the table to help her. She glanced up for a second. Her eyes were red and puffy as if she'd been crying.

"How's your headache? Are you feeling any better?"

She nodded and then shrugged as if she wasn't sure.

"Stella says she'll take you to the hospital tomorrow," I said, picking up one of the last few pieces of the puzzle.

"I expect she'll come by just before three. It was a lovely service today, you know. Mrs. Jackson was proud as anything, and I met Father Hill. He seems nice."

Mum's body gave a sudden jolt as if she'd received an electric shock. The piece of green puzzle she'd been holding flew across the table, landing in my lap. "Hey, what's the matter?" I passed the piece back to her, sorry I'd said anything. Then I remembered that she'd reacted weirdly last time I mentioned Father Hill too. He obviously knew something about Mum's past – maybe he knew about the baby in the photo – and she was scared he was going to spill the beans.

"Are you hungry?" she mumbled, changing the subject. "I could make you an omelette or something..."

"No thanks, I ate loads of cake at the christening. Let's just finish the puzzle, shall we?"

There were only about ten pieces left. We sat in silence, turning them this way and that, trying to work out how they were supposed to fit together. I let Mum put in the final piece since she'd done most of it herself anyway. It looked amazing. The picture spread out across the table like a beautiful work of art.

"We should celebrate or something," I said. "Have a finishing-the-puzzle party! Why don't we order pizza?"

Mum shook her head. "I think I'll just get an early

night, if that's okay with you, Becky. I've got my appointment with the doctor tomorrow and I'm so tired all the time." She kissed the top of my head and trailed upstairs.

"Love you, Mum," I called after her, but I don't think she heard.

I was just about to go up myself when there was a tap on the front door. I could see through the glass that it was Mack. He'd changed into shorts and a T-shirt but he still looked drop-dead gorgeous.

"I've just come round to synchronize watches," he said, grinning. "You know, for our plan tomorrow."

"But you're not wearing a watch," I said, trying not to laugh.

He waved his phone at me. "I actually meant synchronize *phones*, but no one ever says that in a proper spy movie!"

"Except this isn't a spy movie and I never get a good enough signal around here to use my phone anyway."

"Okay, okay, forget the watches and phones," he said, exasperated. "The real reason I came round was to ask you if you're ready for your third swimming lesson. I was going to talk to you about it at the christening but I got distracted by Mrs. Jackson's scones."

I shook my head, the conversation serious suddenly. "I don't think so, Mack. I do want to carry on learning but I just feel weird about it right now, you know, because of..."

"Because of my dad?"

I shrugged, nodding. Actually, I was dying to talk to Colin, to find out exactly what he knew about my dad, but it was just too risky while Mum was so fragile.

"But, Becky, in lesson number three you get to put your face in the water and blow bubbles. It's even better than hopping, trust me."

"I do trust you," I said. "And I promise I'll carry on, just not right now."

Mack turned and started down the path. "I'll keep on asking until you say yes," he said over his shoulder. "I'll go on and on about it. I'll drive you completely nuts until you agree to come just to shut me up."

I smiled to myself in the dark. He was only asking me to go swimming – and I'd probably messed it up anyway by saying no – but he was still the cutest and funniest and nicest guy I'd ever met in my life. I thought about all those times I'd sat in Laura's room, mooning over Jamie Palmer. I bet she'd never believe a boy like Mack could be interested in someone like me. It was difficult to believe it myself.

I set my alarm and left for the Butterfly Garden as early as possible the next morning. I'd promised Rosa May I'd stay all day, but I knew I'd have to get home by three if I was going to take another look at the photo. She was already there when I arrived, waiting for me by the entrance, her face closed up and angry.

"At last!" she muttered. "I can't believe you've actually bothered to show up!"

"I promised, didn't I?"

She was still cross about yesterday, really cross. We linked arms and made our way down towards the lake but she was agitated, pulling me along. "How was the christening then?" she scoffed. "I bet you were bored out of your brains!"

"It was okay," I said tightly.

"What, so going to church to see some baby dressed in a frilly white dress was better than spending the afternoon here with me?"

She was on edge. Ready to pick a fight.

"We've been through this already, Rosa May. I had to go and you could've come with me if you'd wanted to. Can't we change the subject?"

"Fine," she said. "*Whatever*. Who wants to talk about a stupid christening anyway?" She ran ahead, turning cartwheels across the field – one after the other, as if she was in the circus. I lagged behind, watching her. She was so exhausting to be with when she was in a mood like this.

"You'll never guess what," she called back when she'd reached the lake. "I broke my record yesterday. I stayed under water for five minutes without breathing. *Five whole minutes! Do you want to see?*"

I could feel the energy drain out of me. I shook my head, sinking down into the grass, too weak suddenly to walk any further.

"Come and sit here," I said, patting the space next to me. "Don't go in the water. Come here and we'll keep a look out for a Silver-studded Blue."

She skipped back over to me and sat down, cuddling up close, her anger gone in a blink. When she stopped being cross for five minutes she was so lovely to be with, but I knew it wouldn't last. No matter how much time we spent together, she always wanted more.

"I don't think we'll spot one today, to be honest," she said. "I've just got a bad feeling about it."

"What do you mean?"

"Well, maybe we've been looking *too* hard. Running around, searching every area of the Garden. If we really want to spot the first Silver-studded Blue of the summer, we probably need to sit in one place, *all day*, and wait."

"But we've spent days and days lying in the grass, sometimes for hours on end, and we still haven't spotted one."

She shook her head. "But not *all* day. Not from early in the morning until the sun goes down. That's what we need to do if we're serious. You're not rushing off today, are you?"

I shrugged, too weary to explain that I couldn't stay for the whole day. Rosa May shrank back from me. "What's that supposed to mean? Why did you shrug like that? Are you staying or going? You promised me you'd stay all day, remember?"

"Look, I came really early because I've got to get home by three." I paused for a moment, waiting for her reaction, but she didn't say anything. Her eyes were fixed on my face like lasers.

"It's because of the photo," I went on, eager to fill the silence. "Remember the photo? Under my mum's bed? Well, Father Hill said something really weird yesterday – something about how difficult it must be for my mum to be back in Oakbridge – and there's no way I can ask her what he meant, not while she's so ill, but Mack said I should check the photo, you know, check to see if there were any clues I missed the first time I saw it." I was babbling now, unable to stop. "That's why I have to get home, because Mum's going to the hospital at three with Stella so it'll give me a chance to look."

Rosa May's face had turned deathly pale.

"*Mack*," she spat. She wrapped her arms around her body as if she was cold suddenly. "You've been seeing *Mack*."

"Not *seeing* him," I said. "Well, only once or twice but it's not as if he's my boyfriend or anything. He's really nice, Rosa May, and funny. You'd like him, I know you would."

"Why did you lie?" she said, ignoring me. "You swore to me you wouldn't see him again. I trusted you, Becky, but you've betrayed me, just like everyone else."

Her words cut through me. "No I haven't!" I cried. "Please, Rosa May, don't be like this. We're best friends. Mack can't change that. No one could ever come between us. If you liked a boy, I wouldn't mind. I'd be happy for you. *Please*."

She stood up, backing away from me, pressing her fingers to the sides of her head as if she was in pain. It was like looking at Mum.

"Stop it! Don't do that!" I lunged at her, pulling her hands down. "Why are you staring at me like that? *What is it?*"

"Don't you understand, Becky?" Her eyes narrowed. "It's time for you to make a choice."

"*What?*"

"You heard me. It's time to choose. You can't have both of us. It's me or Mack."

The air was thick and heavy, pressing down on me. I reached out for her but she stepped back further. It was difficult to breathe. "*Rosa May!*"

"I mean it, Becky. I'm deadly serious. If you carry on seeing Mack you can forget all about us. If you choose him over me, I don't want to be your friend any more." Her arms were still wrapped around her body like a shield. "I don't want to be your friend and I don't want to see you ever again."

I shook my head, determined to get through to her. "Why are you being like this? We'll always be friends, Rosa May. What about the Silver-studded Blue? What about our pact? You promised me. Don't make me choose, please!"

She'd changed. Something about her was different. I stared into her eyes. They were cold. I could see something there but I couldn't quite work out what it was. And then I realized. It was hate. Rosa May hated me.

Chapter Twenty

I staggered back, gasping for air. I had to get away. I pushed my way through the long grass, looking over my shoulder to make sure she wasn't following. I was scared. Scared of her eyes. Scared of what I'd seen there.

She didn't move from where she was standing. I glanced back one last time before I left. She was a small, blue blur in the distance. Too far away to hurt me. But it wasn't until I was at the top of Amble Cross that I dared to stop for a second and take a proper breath.

I stumbled on, frantic to put as much distance between us as I could. I got as far as the green and collapsed down on the grass. I hugged my knees to my chest, trying to understand how everything had turned so nasty. I couldn't face going home, not while Mum was still there, but I didn't have anywhere else to go. Mrs. Jackson was in her usual spot in the doorway of the shop.

"What's the matter, Becky?" she called out, hurrying over as soon as she saw me. "What's happened? You look dreadful."

I tried to say I was fine but the words were lost as tears started to roll down my face.

"Hey, come on now, my love. What's brought this on?"

I was crying so hard I could barely speak. Mrs. Jackson held out her hands and pulled me up into her arms.

"It's alright," she soothed, stroking my hair. "It might seem like the end of the world but I'm sure we can put things right."

I leaned into her, sobbing. "It's just I've had the most terrible row with my friend. It was horrible, she said all these nasty things and—"

"Now you listen to me, Becky Miller. Friends fall out all the time. You'll be the best of pals again tomorrow, you see if you're not."

I wanted to believe her but I knew she was wrong. I'd seen Rosa May's eyes.

"Let's get out of this frightful heat for a bit, shall we?

I've got some cake left over from yesterday and a few of those scrummy scones." She led me across the green towards the shop. "Do you know, my friend Tilly and I used to fall out more often than we had hot dinners and we're still the best of friends today."

Mr. Jackson was at the till. He'd unclipped the fan and was holding it right up to his face. "There's a storm coming," he said as we trooped past. "You mark my words, heat like this is always followed by a storm."

"He's been saying that every day for the past month," said Mrs. Jackson. "Wishful thinking, that's what I call it!"

We squashed up in the Jacksons' tiny kitchen. Every surface was covered with leftovers from the day before. The plants on the window sill were heaving with juicy red tomatoes, so ripe they looked as if they were about to split open at any moment.

Mrs. Jackson cut me a huge slice of Victoria sponge and we sat together looking through the photos from the christening. Mrs. Jackson's son had dropped them off that morning. There were literally hundreds of Albert in his frilly white dress. Albert with his parents. Albert with his grandparents. Albert with his aunties and uncles and all his cousins. There were toddlers and teenagers and two elderly aunts who were easily over a hundred. I thought of me and Mum – our tiny family of two – and my tummy twisted up.

We had to do this family tree once at school and of course I had nothing to put on mine – it was more like a twig than a tree. Mrs. Pond, my teacher, suggested I ask Mum for a list of all my relatives, but when I asked Mum that evening she said she was too tired. I tried asking her the next morning, but she was busy getting ready for work and she didn't have time. I think she said something like, *For goodness' sake, Becky, why can't they just teach you to add up and spell properly?* And I didn't bother asking her again after that, there didn't seem to be much point. I glanced across at the window sill. If only I could make my family grow as easily as Mrs. Jackson's tomatoes. Perhaps then I wouldn't feel so frightened and alone.

Right at the end, after all the photos of Albert, there was one of me and Mack, our heads close together, talking. It was such a lovely photo. I ran my hand over it, smiling to myself.

"I was only twelve when I met Mr. Jackson," said Mrs. Jackson, her face creasing up. "And I'll tell you what, he gave me the exact same look young Mackie Williams is giving you in that photo. He's smitten, Becky Miller, clear as the nose on my face."

"No he isn't," I said, turning crimson. I pushed the

photo away. And anyway, even if he was, how could I choose between him and Rosa May?

"No go on, take it with you," she said.

I blushed even more as I slipped it into my pocket. "Thank you," I whispered, shyly. "You know, Albert's so lucky to have you as his gran."

As I left the shop my phone vibrated in my pocket. It was a text from Mack: *My mum's just picked up yours. The coast is clear x.* I rushed home and up the stairs to Mum's room. I felt as if I was breaking into my own house, sneaking around like a thief, but I had to find out what Mum was hiding. Like Mack said that day on the way home from the pool, *It's always better to know the truth.*

The box was still there, under her bed. I pulled it out and sat with it on my lap, trying to work up the courage to look inside. "*It's always better to know the truth,*" I whispered to myself. And then, with my eyes half-closed, I lifted the lid, almost in slow motion, as if the whole thing might explode in my hands. But Mum must've remembered more about the day she collapsed than she was letting on, because the box was empty. There was nothing in it. No photo. No tatty piece of fabric with *I LOVE YOU* stitched across the middle. Nothing.

I dropped the box on the bed, my eyes flying round the room. The photo had to be here somewhere. If it was precious enough to keep hidden away for so long, she wouldn't just throw it away. I pulled the drawer out by her bed. There was a book and a packet of tissues and some other bits and pieces. I flicked through the book to see if she'd slipped the photo inside and then turned the whole drawer upside down on the bed, but it wasn't there.

I moved on to the wardrobe, grabbing all her folded tops and giving them a good shake before dropping them on the floor. Where would she hide a photo? It was so small. It could be anywhere. It might even be with her at the hospital, in her handbag or her pocket. I was determined to find it. The last thing I wanted was to make Mum ill again, but I felt as if I'd gone too far to give up now.

She had loads of hanging clothes. All her skirts and jackets from work and a whole load of dresses she never wore but kept anyway, year after year. They were brightly coloured, silky. The kind of dresses Stella wore. I fingered them for a moment, trying to imagine Mum, younger and happier, dressed up to go out. Then I pushed them to one side and crawled inside.

The wardrobe was deeper than I realized and the area behind the hanging clothes was pitch black. I felt around with my hands, as my eyes adjusted to the dark. There didn't seem to be much in there except for a couple of shoeboxes, right at the back, one on top of the other. The first one had a pair of shiny, black high heels. Mum's work shoes. I chucked them to one side and grabbed the second box.

I could tell straight away that there were no shoes inside, even before I opened it. It was old, bulging at the sides, held together with a thick elastic band. I crawled back out of the wardrobe and sat for a moment on the floor, holding the box on my lap. And then before I could change my mind, or chicken out, I removed the band and lifted the dusty lid.

The box was stuffed full of old newspaper cuttings, photos, drawings and a notebook. My breath was coming fast, my stomach churning as if I was at the highest point on a fairground ride, about to plunge down. I picked up the first cutting. The headline screamed out at me in big bold letters:

RISING SWIMMING STAR IN
DROWNING TRAGEDY

I read the article three times but it still didn't make any sense. A local girl had drowned in a lake. It was in a field near Amble Cross. She was a brilliant swimmer but she was showing off, diving in. It was a hot summer and the lake had dried up, the water wasn't as deep as usual and she banged her head on a rock. Her mum was there but she couldn't save her. By the time they dragged her out of the lake it was too late. According to the article, the accident had happened twelve years ago. Two months before I was born. And the girl's name was Rosa May.

Chapter Twenty-one

I read the next cutting, and the next. The facts were right there in black and white, but they wouldn't sink in. Rosa May was twelve. She'd been swimming since the age of two, she'd won countless medals. But the lake wasn't suitable for swimming, it was full of rocks – an accident waiting to happen. There was an inquest, but the coroner returned a verdict of accidental death. The third article was all about the girl's parents. Her mum, Tracy, was heavily pregnant when the accident happened. She was there, but she couldn't swim. Her friend Stella said Tracy would never forgive herself; that she'd feel guilty for the rest of her life.

I wanted to stop reading but I couldn't. I wanted to tear up every single newspaper cutting and rewind the clock to when I was sitting in Mrs. Jackson's kitchen. The Victoria sponge churned over in my stomach, threatening to come up, but I carried on.

The girl's dad was Ben Miller. The article said he'd never forgive himself either. He was supposed to be spending that fateful day with his daughter, but they'd rowed and she'd stormed out of the house. Tracy had followed but Ben was too angry. They'd always been close before, inseparable even, but they hadn't been getting on.

There were photos too. But still I couldn't take it all in. Photos of the lake and of my mum. There was even one of Stella. And there was one photo of Rosa May. It was in every article. The same photo, black and white, grainy and slightly out of focus. She had long, dark hair and flashing eyes. She was wearing a sundress. The same faded sundress *my* Rosa May had been wearing all summer. I squeezed my eyes shut tight for a second as if I could banish the image from my brain.

The notebook was actually a diary. Mum's diary. Page after page filled with her small, neat handwriting. A couple of entries were smudgy and blurred, as if she'd been crying as she wrote them. The diary started in June, the year I was born, and finished in June a year later. I read a random entry, just one, from the middle of the book.

February 1st

It's been the coldest day of the winter so far. The garden was covered in a thick frost when we woke, and Ben said the lake would be frozen. The image of the frozen lake wouldn't leave me. Rosa May frozen in the lake. Of course I know she's not actually in there, not physically, but I wish he hadn't said it. I wanted to take a great big vat of boiling water down to the fields and pour it into the water. Becky must've sensed how I was feeling. She was grisly all day, demanding, clingy. She wouldn't eat her lunch and it was impossible to settle her. Ben lost patience with us in the end and went out. I wanted to run after him, to beg him to stay and help me with the baby, but I knew he'd say no. He didn't come back until after supper. He was freezing, his hands were blue with cold. I'd made him some soup, his favourite, but he didn't want it. How long is he going to punish me?

I was still sitting there with the diary in my hand and the articles strewn around me when I heard Mum come in from the hospital. I listened out for Stella's voice but she was alone. I got up as if I was in a trance, grabbed some of the cuttings and walked downstairs. Mum was standing by the table, running her hand over the finished puzzle. She glanced up when she heard me.

"Who's Rosa May?" I said, not wanting to hear the answer. Her hand flew off the puzzle and up to her face. She stumbled forward, grabbing the back of a chair to steady herself. I held up the articles in my fist. "Who is she?" I demanded. "*Who is she?*"

"I was going to tell you!" cried Mum. She took a step towards me. "That's why we came back here. I was going to tell you everything, but I didn't know how."

"Tell me what?" I said. "Who is she? I saw the photo under your bed. The baby in the pink blanket. Was that Rosa May? And where's my dad? Why have you got all these newspaper cuttings? What do they mean?" The questions burst out of me.

Mum lowered herself onto the chair. "I was going to tell you everything, Becky. That's why I took the job, why we moved back to Oakbridge, but it's been a nightmare. I wanted to do the right thing, for *your* sake, but I felt as if I was grieving all over again."

"*You're talking in riddles!*" I screamed. "*Just tell me. What happened to Rosa May. Who is she?*"

"Not *is*," said Mum, her voice breaking. "*Was*. She was my daughter. My beautiful daughter." Tears welled in her eyes and started to roll down her face.

I shook my head, totally bewildered. "I don't understand what you're saying. Rosa May's my friend. She can't be your daughter. She's my friend." I felt heavy. Weighed down with confusion. It was like knowing but not knowing.

Mum seemed to fold in on herself. "Stop it," she sobbed. "Stop it. She's not your friend. Don't say that."

"It's true. I'll prove it to you. I've been meeting her every day at the Butterfly Garden. She's my best friend. We've been searching for the Silver-studded Blue. I've got photos of her. Loads of photos. I'll show you."

I thought she was going to pass out. "*Stop it!*" she screamed. "*Stop saying that. You haven't been meeting her. You haven't got photos. She's dead.*" She covered her ears with her hands, but I couldn't stop.

"No she's not. She can't be." I dropped the cuttings and pulled out my phone. "Look, I'll show you! I'll *prove* it to you!" But I realized then, somewhere deep inside, that she wouldn't be in the photos. I knew, but I had to look anyway – to prove it to *myself*. I scrolled up and down, my fingers slipping on the screen. All those photos I'd taken of Rosa May...searching for ants, diving into the lake, tiptoeing round Butterfly Rock...they were all there

– the ants, the lake, the rock – but Rosa May wasn't in them. Not a single one. It was as if she'd been erased.

"Why didn't you tell me?" I whispered, frightened now. "Why did you keep her secret for so long?" I stared at Mum, the awful, heart-wrenching truth seeping through my body like poison. All the little things that didn't add up. The fact that I never once saw Rosa May outside of the Garden, that I never saw her eat, or met her dad or anyone else she knew. The way Maggie and Jean kept commenting on how nice it would be for me to have a friend; how concerned they seemed.

"I've got to go to her," I said weakly. "She'll be waiting for me on the bridge."

Mum tried to grab me. "Stop it," she said again. "Rosa May is dead. She was my beautiful girl but I couldn't save her. I tried, God knows I tried, but I couldn't."

I pushed her away as hard as I could. "*But she's still there!*" I screamed. "*And she needs me! You don't understand anything!*" I was so angry I wanted to lash out, hurt her. "*Why didn't you save her? WHY DID YOU LET HER DIE?*" I lunged at the puzzle suddenly, clawing at it, messing it up. "This is all you care about!" I flung the pieces of the puzzle at her, one handful after the other. The sky, the fields, the bright red poppies.

Mum tried to grab hold of me again but I shoved her

out of the way, snatched back one of the articles, and ran out of the house.

I didn't stop once the whole way to the Garden. It was scorching hot, the sun a blazing ball in the sky. I could hear Mum calling after me but I didn't look back. I had to see Rosa May. To touch her. To tell her how much I loved her. She was waiting for me on the bridge. I could see her from the entrance. Relief coursed through me as I raced across the field.

"I knew you'd be back," she called out as I got closer. Her arms were still folded stiffly across her chest as if she hadn't moved since I left the Garden earlier. "I knew you'd choose me over Mack."

I stumbled onto the bridge, waving the cutting. "Look," I said. "I found this article hidden away in my mum's wardrobe." I bent over double, trying to catch my breath, scared to look at her, scared of what I might see. "I know what happened. I know everything."

Rosa May gasped. She grabbed my arm and snatched the article out of my hand, flinging it in the water. Her eyes were wild, full of fury.

"Let go!" I said, but she dug her nails deeper into my wrist. "Let *go*, Rosa May, you're hurting me."

"So now you know," she said, pushing her face into mine.

"Please, Rosa May..."

"Now you know all about your big sister. The *forgotten* sister! The one who was left in the lake!"

"It wasn't like that." I felt weak in her grip. I tried to lift my arm, to pull it away, but she was too strong.

"Who do you think you are anyway?" she hissed. "Stealing my mum away from me, stealing my *life*." Her face was touching mine. It was twisted up, full of hate.

"You said your mum was dead. Why did you say that? None of this makes any sense. *None of it.*"

"She's as good as dead to me," she spat. "She left me in the water. She put you first, didn't she? Her precious unborn baby. She *abandoned* me." She tightened her grip. "*Why should you get to go out with boys? Start a new school? Live the life that I was supposed to live? What do you think it's been like for me, trapped here for all these years? Trapped for twelve long, lonely years, while you've been out there living my life.*" Her voice was softer suddenly. "But it doesn't matter any more, does it, Becky? Because we're together now. You're going to stay here with me like a good girl."

"What do you mean?" She was still gripping my wrist. "You're hurting me."

"Becky and Rosa May. Together at last. I've been waiting for you for such a long time."

"Let go, Rosa May," I pleaded. "I don't understand. You're really scaring me."

"*Becky!*" Mum was suddenly at the top of the field.

"*Mum!*" I tried to loosen Rosa May's grip but she twisted my arm behind my back and bundled me off the bridge down to the other side of the lake.

"*Becky!*" Mum screamed. "*Get away from the lake.*"

I tried but I couldn't. Rosa May was dragging me towards the edge. Pulling me along, forcing me into the water.

"You'll never be able to leave me now," she said, wrapping her arms right round me.

"Stop it," I gasped. "I can't swim." The water was icy cold. The air flew out of my lungs. "Let go of me, Rosa May, please!"

Her voice was soft in my ear. "I told you I'd find a way to make the summer last for ever."

I tried to dig my heels in, to push back against her, but it was useless. She was so much stronger than me. I felt limp in her arms. Helpless. She dragged me in deeper, down into the lake, until the water closed over my head.

Chapter Twenty-two

It was cold and dark. Rosa May's hair swirled around us in the silence. Weird pictures filled my head, playing out like a film...Rosa May, that first day she jumped in front of me, hands on her hips. Mack and I sitting in his den, playing noughts and crosses. Mr. Jackson's crossword. Mum's puzzle, broken up into hundreds of pieces. And my dad. I could see my dad, but I was little, maybe two, and he was holding me in his arms, keeping me safe.

A sound penetrated the silence. It was my name, muffled, far away. I heard it again. I kicked my legs, pushing my body up towards the sound, but Rosa May held me down. I kicked harder, straining to reach the voice, and we shot up, breaking the surface. The light was blinding. The air rushed into my lungs. I saw Mum – she was at the edge of the lake, screaming my name. The sound seemed to fill the entire Garden. Her voice was clear but her face was blurred. I tried to call out for help, but before I could form the words I was back underwater.

Panic filled every part of my brain; the pictures were gone. Rosa May was facing me now. I kicked again, harder, twisting my body away from her. My arms were free. I pushed against her, thrashing at the water. We rose up once more. I gulped at the air, looking for Mum, but she'd gone. Terror shot through me. I tried to swivel round, to see if she was further along the bank, but Rosa May's grip was like iron and in seconds I was under again.

My mind was blank now. Rosa May's arms tightened around me and after a few more feeble kicks I surrendered. It was calm, peaceful. The water was full of bubbles. There was something about bubbles – something Mack had said – but I couldn't remember what it was and the thought dissolved in the water, floating away. I was drowsy, drifting off. No strength left to reach for the light above.

I heard a sound. The water moved around me, knocking against me, gentle at first, then rough. More sounds in the distance, too far away to mean anything. But then arms grabbing me; desperate, grasping arms, dragging me up to the light.

"*Becky!*"

It was Mum. Holding me. Pulling me.

"*Becky, look at me. I've got you. Becky, open your eyes. Wake up, Becky! Wake up!*"

Mum? In the water? Shaking me. I struggled to clear my head.

"*Hold onto me, Becky. Help me. It's not deep. Come on, Becky. We're almost out. Come on!*"

More arms. Hauling me up. Rolling me over. Light. Cold. Air.

I gasped, desperate for air. Big breaths. Deep, gulping breaths.

"Oh, Becky!" Mum was lying over me, sobbing. "I'm so sorry. I'm so, so sorry."

"Mum?" My voice was hoarse, barely a whisper. "Mum, I'm so cold." My mouth filled up with water and I leaned over, coughing.

"Becky! Oh thank god! I thought I'd lost you. I couldn't bear it. I couldn't live with myself. Not again."

I clung on to her, still coughing. She was cold as well, shivering. Did she come in the water? Did she save me? There were other people, crowded round, leaning over.

"It's okay," said Mum. "Thank you for your help, but we're okay now."

She pulled me tight, rocking me against her as the faces melted away.

My body felt heavy, weighed down. I tried to take a deep breath, but I didn't have the strength. We sat there, rocking, both of us too shocked to speak.

"What were you *doing*, Becky?" Mum said in the end. "What were you thinking?"

"It was Rosa May, Mum," I croaked, my voice still hoarse. "She wanted me to come in the water. She's been begging me to swim with her all summer, practically every day, but I was too scared. I've had a few lessons with Mack but I didn't dare swim with Rosa May. She was wild, Mum. She would dive into the lake and stay under for ages. I hated it." I struggled to sit up, terrified suddenly. "Where is she now? Is she still in the lake?"

"No, Becky," Mum sobbed. "Please. There's no Rosa May. Rosa May died a long time ago."

"I don't understand it either, Mum, but she's in there, I swear. I know she's dead, I get it, but she's still in the lake. How long was I in the water? Two minutes? Three? Any second now, you'll see." I scanned the surface. It was completely still, but I knew her tricks.

"I'm serious, Mum." I didn't know how to make her

believe me. "She dragged me in. You *must've* seen her. We've been together all summer, hanging out here, searching for the Silver-studded Blue. She told me about the ancient myth, that if you're the first to spot a Silver-studded Blue then the person you love the most is on their way to see you, but if it lands on your shoulder then that person has come to say goodbye for ever..."

"*Stop it*, Becky! You're rambling..."

"No I'm not, it's all true. We were so close, but she didn't want me to be friends with Mack. She was jealous. She wanted me all to herself." I tried to get up, thrashing against Mum, frantic, but she pulled me back down. "Let go of me. *Let go!* We've got to find her!"

"No, Becky!" Mum tightened her arms around me so that I couldn't move. "An ambulance is on its way. You've got to rest. Rosa May is *not* in the water. She died a long, long time ago. She's not here. You're safe."

I shook my head, still straining to see the lake. She was wrong. I could feel Rosa May watching, waiting. "But I don't understand," I said. "I don't understand anything."

Mum stroked my hair. "It's all my fault, I should've told you the truth right from the start. I made a terrible mistake. Your dad wanted me to tell you, so did Stella – they said you had a right to know, that it was the right thing to do – but I couldn't bring myself to talk about it.

I kept everything to show you, all the clippings and photos, but every time I tried to form the words, my head would start throbbing. I *wanted* to tell you, but I just couldn't."

"Tell me now," I said weakly. "Tell me everything. But please, Mum, you must believe me. She *is* here."

I leaned into her, safe for the minute, and she began to talk.

Chapter Twenty-three

"Rosa May was always larger than life," Mum started. "She was so different from your dad and me, we used to joke that they must've got her mixed up at the hospital, given us the wrong baby. She was bright and beautiful, perfect really, but she was in such a hurry to grow up. She wanted to run before she could walk. We struggled to keep up, to be honest. We were very young – I was only eighteen when I had her – but even so, she was always one step ahead of us and it was exhausting at times.

"She was brilliant at everything she did, but swimming was her passion. She was swimming by the age of two, you know. Your dad called her Fish. She swam for her school and for the county. They even said she might swim in the Olympics one day.

"We were so proud of her, Becky, she was doing so well, but then we found out we were expecting you. Rosa May was almost twelve by then, in her first year of secondary school and we thought she'd be thrilled. She'd been begging us for a sister for years, but we'd always joked that having her was like having a houseful of children already! We couldn't wait to tell her – a sister at last – but she didn't take it well at all. She was horribly jealous, convinced that we'd love the baby more than her. That we wouldn't have enough love to share round."

She stopped for a moment, hugging me close. I could sense Rosa May listening. Taking in every word. I couldn't see her but I knew she was there.

"She started to act out," Mum went on. "Picking fights with us, pushing the boundaries, staying out late without telling us where she was. She'd always been so driven, so determined to do well, but she began to miss her training. She said she couldn't be bothered any more. Your dad really struggled with that. They'd always been so close and he was so proud of her. He couldn't understand where his lovely little girl had gone. It broke his heart."

"She told me how close they were," I said, looking up at Mum. "She said they had a special connection."

Mum took a deep, shaky breath and carried on as if I hadn't spoken.

"Things got worse as the pregnancy went on. Perhaps we'd spoiled her, being an only child for so long. Or maybe it was just one change too many, after just starting secondary school and everything...I don't know. I've tried to analyze it so many times, to understand why she found it so difficult to accept. She began to stay out for hours on end. She'd be down here by the lake, hanging out on her own. There was no Butterfly Garden back then, just some fields with the lake in the middle.

"That day, the day of the accident, she was supposed to be competing in a swimming gala. We'd planned to take her, cheer her on, but the doctor was worried about me. My blood pressure was high. He said he wanted me to go to the hospital for some tests and a scan and he scheduled it for that day. Stella offered to go and watch Rosa May instead, but she went mad. She said she didn't want Stella, that we were putting the new baby first already. There was an almighty row and she stormed out.

"Your dad refused to go after her. He said he was tired of all the arguments. Worn out. But I came down here, to the fields, to see if I could talk her round. When she saw me, she started to play up even more, showing off, teasing me about how pathetic it was that I couldn't swim.

"'*Come and get me*,' she kept taunting, and then she'd dive in the lake and stay under until I was frantic with worry. When she came up, she'd laugh as if it was the biggest joke. I begged her to come out of the water, to come home. I promised we'd change the hospital appointment, go for the scan the next day, that she could come with us, see her new baby sister. And finally she calmed down. She climbed out of the lake and we started to walk back, holding hands. I remember squeezing her hand – she squeezed mine back and I really thought at that moment that everything was going to be okay. She was going through a tough time, a bad patch, that was all. But then she turned round.

"'*One more dive!*' she shouted, running back towards the lake. I'll never forget the sight of her tearing through the grass, her beautiful hair flying out behind her. I've been haunted by that moment for the past twelve years. It was the last time I saw her alive. She dived into the water, half twisting round to make sure I was watching. It put her off her stride, she went in at an awkward angle. She must've hit her head on a rock. It all happened so fast.

"I didn't realize at first. I thought she was up to her usual antics, staying under to give me a fright. I waited and waited. It felt like hours...and then it dawned on me that something was wrong. That she wasn't coming up.

I was all alone, Becky, I didn't know what to do. I ran down to the edge of the lake and lowered myself into the water. It was so cold, colder than anything I'd ever experienced. I tried to move towards her but my feet got tangled in the weeds. They were everywhere, snaking round my legs, dragging me down. I could feel myself sinking. I tried to steady myself, pull my feet free, but I was so huge and heavy it was impossible.

"Everything went dark for a moment. I was fighting for breath. I could see where she was but I couldn't reach her. Too much time was passing. It was a nightmare. I called out to her, told her to hang on, that everything was going to be okay, but she wasn't moving. She was too still. I screamed at her to move – I knew I was losing her. I screamed and screamed. That's the last thing I remember before I lost consciousness.

"I woke up in hospital. They told me a man had been out walking his dog, near to the lake. He didn't actually see Rosa May dive in, but he heard me screaming. He was very strong; a confident swimmer. He managed to haul me out, but by the time he got to Rosa May, by the time more help arrived – the ambulance and paramedics – it was too late."

Her voice broke and she hugged me tighter, rocking me back and forth.

"Poor Rosa May," I said, shuddering. "All alone in the water. She must've been so cold."

"At first we each blamed ourselves," said Mum. "Your dad thought it was his fault for not following her after the row, but I knew it was mine for not saving her when I had the chance. I replayed those moments in the water over and over, as if they were stuck in my brain on some awful loop. We tore ourselves apart. It was like all the lights had gone out. You were the only thing that kept us going, Becky, the thought of a new life.

"You came two weeks after the funeral; the midwife said it was the stress. You came so fast there was no time to get your dad. He was down here by the lake. He spent every day here; sometimes he even slept here, all night, by the lake. He tried to come to terms with what had happened but he couldn't. He went a bit mad, to tell you the truth. Mad with grief. He started to blame me. He said I'd put our unborn baby before Rosa May."

I twisted round to look at Mum. "But that's what Rosa May said on the bridge. She said you chose me over her. She hates me, you know."

Mum cupped her hands around my face. "Please, Becky. I want you to listen to what I'm saying. There *is* no Rosa May – not any more. It's been a difficult time for you. Moving to Oakbridge, spending so much time alone, all these weeks with nothing to do – it's unsettled you. It's my fault. I should've noticed things weren't right but I've been so wrapped up in my own grief and misery. Being back here must've triggered off some old memories in you – things you overheard us say when you were a little girl, before your dad left."

"So is that what happened?" I asked, desperately trying to follow Mum's story. "Is that when my dad left?"

"He couldn't cope, Becky. He loved you, but it was difficult for him to be with you. It wasn't your fault. It was just too much – a new baby when he'd just lost his precious Rosa May. He set up a fund in her memory. He wanted to build a memorial, but the idea grew into this place, the Butterfly Garden. He organized it all himself. He was so immersed in it, he didn't have time for us. There was this rock – the butterflies loved it because the stone was so warm. He said it was the only place he felt close to her. The only place he wanted to be."

"Butterfly Rock," I murmured.

"Yes, that's right. Butterfly Rock; or 'Rosa May's Rock', as he began to call it. I couldn't come to the Garden myself – it was too painful – but he couldn't stay away. We argued night and day. I wanted him to spend more time with me, more time with *us*, but when I asked him, he would stare right through me as if I wasn't there.

"He did try to take you swimming a few times, at the leisure centre, but you hated it. He forced you to go in but you'd scream blue murder. He didn't understand. He wanted you to be like Rosa May. One day I heard him calling you his 'little Rosa May', and that's when it all blew up. We had the most terrible row and he said he couldn't carry on, that he was going away. He went travelling, all the way to Australia. His family were already living there – his parents and his sister – so that's where he stayed."

There was a huge lump in my throat; it was totally clogged up. No wonder the pool felt so familiar... But the thought of Dad wishing I was Rosa May, it was just so sad.

"What about us?" I said. "When did we leave Oakbridge?"

"Not long after that. You were about two-and-a-half. I needed a fresh start. I couldn't cope with all the memories and everyone knowing. You know what it's like around here. I knew what people were thinking – how could a mother let her own child drown? But I swear to you, Becky, I did everything I could to save her. And I kept meaning to tell you, but the more time went by, the harder it became. I wanted to protect you from the past. I didn't want you to feel as if you were growing up in Rosa May's shadow – or to blame yourself for what happened."

"Is that where he is then?" I whispered. "My dad? In Australia?"

Mum took a deep, shaky breath. "That's where he was until a few months ago, but he's on his way home, Becky. He wrote to me shortly before we moved, to say he was planning to come back to Oakbridge and that he wanted to see you. That's why I came back. I wanted to give you both a chance to get to know each other properly. I had this idea that if we were living here too, then perhaps we could be a family again. I thought enough time had passed, that I was strong enough to face up to what happened, but I've found it so painful."

My mouth dropped open. My dad was on his way home to see me.

"I can hear the ambulance," said Mum, twisting round to look over her shoulder. "They'll need to check you over. You've had a terrible shock."

Two men came running across the field, carrying a big bag. They told me their names were Nathan and Danny. They wrapped me in a blanket and asked me loads of questions, but it was impossible to concentrate. I didn't need to spot the Silver-studded Blue after all. My dad was coming home.

"They want us to go down to the hospital," said Mum, helping me to my feet. "Just to make sure your lungs are okay, that you didn't take in too much water."

I shook her arm off. "I'm sorry, but I've got to find Rosa May first." Mum opened her mouth but she didn't say anything. "I mean it, Mum. I'm not leaving until I've said goodbye."

I sensed she was there before I turned round. She was on the bridge, watching us. She looked different. Faded. As if the lake had finally drained the life out of her. I wasn't scared any more. I knew she couldn't hurt me. I understood. She'd never meant to hurt me in the first place; she was just lonely and angry. Angry that her life had been cut so short.

"I'm here, Rosa May," I said, shrugging off the blanket, running onto the bridge. Running towards my big sister. I put my arms around her and pulled her close, stroking her hair. I thought of the photo, of Rosa May as a newborn baby wrapped in that pink blanket, and I pulled her even closer.

"I'm sorry we didn't find the Silver-studded Blue," she whispered.

"It doesn't matter. We found each other instead."

"I love you, Becky. I never meant to frighten you. I just wanted you to stay with me. I've been so lonely."

"I love you too. I'll always love you. So does Mum. She never stopped loving you, not for one second."

"I know," she wept, silent tears coursing down her face. "I heard her."

We stood on the bridge, clinging onto each other for the last time. She felt light, as if the air could pass right through her. She was disappearing, slipping away.

Mum took a step towards me. "Come on, Becky, the ambulance is waiting," she called.

"I've got to go," I said, holding her even tighter.

She laced her fingers through mine so that it was impossible to see where her hands started and mine ended. "Thank you, Becky. Thank you for this summer, for helping me. I'll never forget you."

"I'll never forget you either, Rosa May."

Mum came up behind me then. She put her hand on my shoulder and led me down off the bridge. I looked back but Rosa May was gone. There was a small splash and then a ripple. It spread right across the lake.

"Bye-bye, Fish," I whispered. "I love you."

Chapter Twenty-four

Once Mum started talking, she didn't stop, like a switch had been flipped. She talked all the way to the hospital and all the way back, and the more she talked, the more animated she became. She'd spent the last ten years keeping everything locked up inside – she said it was the only way she could cope with the pain. But as she told the story of those awful years, it was as if she was slowly coming back to life.

They kept us at the hospital for ages. They were worried that Mum wasn't well enough to look after me; they said they were concerned for my welfare. Pam was there and she wanted to know how I'd ended up in the water in the first place when I couldn't swim. I didn't tell them about Rosa May. I didn't say much at all; I left all the talking to Mum, and she somehow managed to convince them that we'd be okay.

"I know I've let you down," she said on the way home. "Keeping Rosa May secret, hiding everything from you – it was the worst thing I could've done."

"You didn't know," I said. "You were only trying to do what you thought was best at the time. But there is one thing I don't understand. Didn't I ask you about my dad after he left? Didn't I wonder where he was?"

Mum sighed. "Of course you did. You asked every day for a while – it broke my heart. But then we moved ourselves, and you started nursery, made new friends, and it was as if you'd left him behind. You stopped asking where he was and when he was coming back, and then one day I heard you tell one of your friends that you'd never met your daddy. Explaining that you *had* met him, but that he'd left you, just felt too cruel. I know it was wrong now, *so* wrong, but it seemed the kindest way at the time."

The house was a state, especially the kitchen. There were newspaper cuttings and pieces of puzzle everywhere. It was hard to believe that only a few hours earlier we'd been standing there screaming at each other. It seemed like ages ago, days even.

"I'm sorry about the puzzle," I said. "I didn't know what I was doing. I was so scared and angry."

Mum turned me round by the shoulders and led me out of the kitchen. "Please don't say sorry, Becky. I don't care about the puzzle. I only started doing them after Rosa May died as a way of numbing the pain, but I don't need to do that any more. I'm going to make you a hot, sweet drink and tuck you up in bed and then I'm going to get this mess cleared up."

I had the best sleep I'd had since moving to Oakbridge. I didn't dream about Rosa May or my dad, but in a weird sort of way I felt they were both close by. My dad was due back in Oakbridge any day, and I realized, as I lay there, that my falling-asleep dream might actually turn into reality. "*Becky Miller, I've been searching for you for the last twelve years!*" I whispered to myself in the dark. *It's okay, Dad, better late than never, eh?*

I woke to the smell of bacon and eggs.

"Morning, sleepyhead," Mum said when I went down. "It's nearly midday, you know. I'm so pleased you slept in. You really needed it."

The kitchen was spotless. Mum had opened all the windows and she was standing at the stove, wearing one of her pretty summer dresses.

"You know, I've been thinking." She handed me a plate

piled high with food. "Why don't you invite Laura up to stay? Maybe next weekend? Or the weekend after that?"

"I'm not sure, Mum. I haven't heard from her all that much since we got here."

Mum sat down at the table with me. "Well, have a think about it and let me know. I can call her mum if you'd like? Oh, and when you've finished eating there are some things I want to show you. In my bedroom."

Mum had laid out a whole load of stuff on her bed. There was the wooden jewellery box, the diary I'd found in the shoebox, some photos and a letter. She opened the jewellery box first and pressed the tatty piece of fabric into my hands.

"I want you to have this," she said. "Rosa May made it for me when she was ten. For Mother's Day. I thought she'd forgotten, you see. The whole day passed and she didn't give me a card, or make a fuss of me, or even say Happy Mother's Day. I was quite hurt. I remember I said to your dad that just a card would've been nice, but then when I went up to bed I found this lying on my pillow. She'd waited all day to surprise me. That was just typical of her." Her eyes filled with tears but she picked up the diary, determined to carry on.

"This is my diary," she said. "I wrote it after you were born, every day for the first year of your life. It's not easy reading, to be honest, and I'm not suggesting you look at it now, but it's here if you ever want to know more about those early days."

I didn't tell her that I'd already read that one awful entry. "What's this?" I asked, picking up the letter.

"It's from your dad. It only came a few weeks ago, just after I lost my job. I was going to give it to you, Becky, but I knew I had to tell you about Rosa May first and I'm so sorry, but I didn't feel strong enough."

I ran my hand over the letter. It was still sealed. "Is it for me? Did he write it to me?"

"Yes, my love, it's for you. I don't know what's in it, I haven't read it."

I looked up at Mum. "Stella said my dad was a lovely man. She said he was gentle and that he cared about animals."

The tears spilled over then, running down Mum's face.

"Oh, he was," she said. "He was wonderful, the only man I've ever loved, but losing a child can do terrible things to you, Becky."

We sat there on the bed with our arms around each other. I wasn't angry with Mum any more; I knew she'd done the best she could. "You know what I'd really like to do?" I said after a bit, pulling back. "It might be hard for you, but I'd like to visit Rosa May's grave."

Mum reached for a tissue from her bedside table and wiped her eyes.

"No, I think that would be lovely," she said. "It's something I should've done a long time ago and it'll be so much easier going with you."

We visited the cemetery later that day. Rosa May's grave was tucked away in a dark, shady corner under a big oak tree. It looked sad, uncared for, forgotten. We'd brought some cutters with us and some lovely fresh flowers and we got busy trimming the grass. Mum told me about the funeral, about how she'd been too ill to attend. She said it was one of her biggest regrets. Father Hill had come round later that day to try and comfort her. He said Rosa May was one of God's angels now and that wherever she was she'd understand, but Mum felt as if she'd let her down all over again.

"Is that why you didn't want to go to Albert's christening?" I asked.

Mum nodded. "I didn't want to see Father Hill again. I was too scared – frightened of what he might say."

"What about Mrs. Wilson? Did she live in Oakbridge back then?"

"No I told you, Becky. I'd never met Mrs. Wilson before that day she came round."

"But she always looks at me as if she *knows*."

Mum sat back on her knees. "Knows what?" she said.

"Oh, I don't know. You've seen her face. It's so sour..."

"Well, she hasn't got the friendliest face in the world," said Mum, smiling, "but I wouldn't read too much into it if I was you."

"Hey, you'll never guess what Mack said. He said Mrs. Wilson performs exorcisms. You know, like in horror movies, when they go into people's houses to get rid of bad spirits and stuff like that!"

Mum's face grew sad again. She glanced down at Rosa May's grave, shaking her head. "There are no bad spirits around here, Becky. Just peace at last for a very special girl whose life was cut short."

I kept expecting Mum to slip back, put herself to bed, clam up, but it didn't happen. She spent the next few days applying for jobs, phoning companies, sending out her CV. She cooked me proper meals, kept the house tidy, and at the end of the week we went to visit my new school. It was on the outskirts of Farnsbury, not far from the leisure centre. We went on the bus and I told Mum all about my swimming lessons with Mack and how determined I was to learn. I was sure she'd freak out, but she was all for it.

She even said she might see about having some lessons herself.

I didn't open the letter from my dad straight away. I never found out who wrote that first note way back at the beginning of the summer, but this was a real letter from my dad and I was frightened. What if it said something awful, like he'd decided to stay in Australia, or that he was coming back but he didn't want to see me after all? It was Stella who persuaded me in the end. She dropped by to see us a few days after everything happened.

"I've been dying to give you this for so long," she said, handing me an old photo. "I found it tucked away in an album from years ago, but your mum didn't want me to show you. Not until she'd told you about Rosa May."

It was a picture of me and my dad outside the Butterfly Garden. It was difficult to see his face very clearly because he was holding me in his arms and we were smiling at each other. I was wearing a little pink sundress and a pink bonnet and I was clasping hold of my dad, my plump baby arms wrapped around his neck.

"This was the day the Butterfly Garden opened," Stella explained. "It was exactly a year after Rosa May died and the opening was supposed to be a celebration of her life."

"What do you mean, 'supposed to be'?" I said, still staring at the photo. At me in my dad's arms.

"He couldn't cope," said Mum quietly. "Everyone was there. All our friends from the village, Rosa May's friends from school, Stella, Colin and Mack, the Jacksons, Father Hill. They'd all turned out to pay their respects, but your dad had a funny turn."

"What happened? What sort of funny turn?"

"He thought he saw Rosa May, in the water. He waded in to try and rescue her, screaming for help. He even called 999. It was awful. We couldn't get him out. We tried to calm him down, we did everything we could, but he was convinced she was in there."

"Maybe she *was*," I said quietly, but Mum had turned to Stella and they were lost in the past, talking about that day at the Garden, the day my dad saw Rosa May in the lake.

I ran up to my room, clutching the photo to my heart, and threw myself across the bed. The letter was under my pillow. I pulled it out and tore it open. It was quite short, only a page, written on thick, white paper.

My dearest Becky,
It's very difficult to write this letter after so much time has passed. Your mum has probably told you that I'm coming home and I'd like you to know that my deepest wish is to see

you again. There's so much I want to talk to you about, to explain. After Rosa May died, I tried to be a father to you, the father you deserved, but I kept getting it wrong. My heart was broken, Becky, and I couldn't fix it. But things have changed. I had to go very far away to learn that the place I most wanted to be was back with you.

I'll understand if you don't want to see me. We can never get those years back, and I'm sure, to start with, I'll seem like a stranger to you. But I'm hoping that, over time, we can get to know each other again.

I'm due back in England at the beginning of September, but I'll wait to hear from you before I contact you again.

I'm sending you an ocean of love in the meantime,

Dad x

Chapter Twenty-five

I only went back to the Butterfly Garden once more before the end of the summer. Mack came with me and we sat on a bench by the lake, chatting. The weather was changing. It was still hot, but heavy clouds filled the sky, blotting out the sun for the first time in weeks. Stella had told Mack about what happened – about Rosa May drowning and how I was going to meet my dad when he came back – but we didn't really talk about it.

"They said it's going to rain later today," I said. "D'you know, I don't even remember what rain looks like, it's been so long!"

"It's wet," said Mack, grinning. "Which reminds me,

are you ready for your next swimming lesson?"

"Do you still want to teach me?" I asked shyly, glancing up at him. I still couldn't get over the fact that he wanted to hang out with me.

"Are you kidding?" he said. "It's bubbles, remember. Bubbles is the best lesson ever!"

"Yeah, okay, but what comes *after* bubbles? It's not actual swimming, is it?"

"Listen, Becky, they're not called *swimming* lessons for nothing. At some point you are going to have to *do* some actual swimming. But don't worry, I'll be there to save you if anything happens. I'll even give you the kiss of life if I have to!"

I could feel myself turning crimson and I looked away, willing my face to cool down. How could he do that? How could he mention kissing? I was just about to suggest we go for a walk, or get something to eat – anything to change the subject – when I spotted a blue butterfly hovering over the bridge. It was different from any of the blue butterflies Rosa May and I had seen before; smaller, more delicate.

"Look," I breathed.

"What?" said Mack.

"Look, over there. That blue butterfly. I think it might be a Silver-studded Blue. I'm not sure, but there's something about it..."

Mack started to ask me what I was on about, but I put my hand on his arm.

"Shhh, don't move."

The butterfly danced towards us, weaving its way through the tall grass, flitting from flower to flower. As it got closer, I saw it was deep blue, with delicate silver edging around its wings. My heart started to thump in my chest.

"It's her," I whispered.

Mack reached for my hand and I held my breath as the butterfly fluttered above our heads. The memories came flooding back...early morning hunts through the bell heather. The first time I saw Butterfly Rock. Lying in the grass with Rosa May as she told me about the ancient myth.

"It's okay," I said, smiling as the butterfly fluttered down, settling on my shoulder. "It's Rosa May, but she's just come to say goodbye."

We sat there for a while longer and watched as the Silver-studded Blue danced its way back over the bridge, disappearing out of sight. We were still sitting there when the first drops of rain fell. We turned our faces up to the sky, almost giddy with excitement, and then, with almost no warning at all, the clouds burst open.

"Come on!" cried Mack, leaping up. "It's time to go!"

And we ran laughing, hand in hand, towards the exit.

Acknowledgements

A really big thank you to: Rebecca Hill, for believing in Becky and Rosa May, but most of all for believing in me; the rest of the team at Usborne for taking so much care over every aspect of the manuscript; my wonderful agent Julia Churchill; my sister Paula for all her brilliant help with the first draft – I swear she was an editor in another life; my mum for letting me talk through the story over and over until I was sure I'd got it right; Callum and Freddy for reading the entire manuscript chapter by chapter as I wrote it, urging me to hurry up so they could find out what happened next. And my BIGGEST thank you of all to Danny, for giving me the self belief I so badly needed to put pen to paper in the first place.

About the author

Anne-Marie Conway is a primary school teacher specializing in drama, who also runs her own children's theatre company, Full Circle. She lives in London with her husband, two young sons and two eccentric cats, Betty and Boo. Anne-Marie's first book, *Phoebe Finds Her Voice*, was picked for the 2011 Summer Reading Challenge.

"Tackling issues of family and friendship,
it's warm and accessible and spot on for the
Cathy Cassidy market."
The Bookseller on *Phoebe Finds Her Voice*

Find out more about Anne-Marie at
www.annemarieconway.com